More praise for *Chasing Saint George* . .

In *Chasing Saint George*, Stephen Murabito creates a cast of rich, memorable characters. While these stories sparkle with small everyday wonders and mysteries, loves and desires, they're also operatic in the best sense of the word, soaring with grand, genuine passion. Murabito tells his tales with great warmth and humor, and with a big, big heart.
—Jim Daniels, author of *Having a Little Talk With Capital P Poetry*

Stephen Murabito, in his beautiful book of stories, *Chasing Saint George*, fleshes out a world of impressionistic operatic sweep that evokes nonetheless the heartbreaking sepia of the documentarian. Murabito's prowess as a poet is evident in every syllable. His ear is exquisite, his attention to detail and nuance utterly precise. *Chasing Saint George* is a book of practiced wit, abiding love, the tattered glory of ordinary unforgettable people engaged in their daily, often absurd, yet absolutely necessary rituals. What happens to them is astonishing. That Murabito has seen them so clearly and delivered them to us with such unflinching clear-eyed devotion is even more so.
—Joseph Bathanti, author of *Restoring Sacred Art*

CHASING SAINT GEORGE

CHASING SAINT GEORGE

Stephen Murabito

Chasing Saint George
© 2010 by Stephen Murabito

cover design: Lucy Swerdfeger

Published by

~Star Cloud Press®~
6137 East Mescal Street
Scottsdale, Arizona 85254-5418

ISBN:

978-1-932842-50-0 — $ 19.95

StarCloudPress.com

Library of Congress Control Number: 2010937211

Printed in the United States of America

Acknowledgments

I thank the readers and editors of the following periodicals, where these stories first appeared (some in slightly different form): "Chasing Saint George" and "The Cooking Lessons," *North American Review*; "My Mother Is a Rosary Lady," *Antietam Review*; "The Stain," *Caketrain*; "Something Bigger, Something Heroic," *Lake Effect*; "Katarina Sistellinos and Big Dave Bates," *Brooklyn Review*; "The Sammy Hall of Fame," *Voices in Italian Americana*; "She Left with the Bear," *Sou'wester*; "Words of Wisdom," *Pittsburgh Quarterly On-line*; "The Run," *Paper Street*; and "The Man Without Any Sins," *The Fourth River*.

"The Stain" also is reprinted in the e-book re-release of *Caketrain* Issue 01, which is available at Caketrain.com.

The two sources for the Grateful Dead lyrics in "The Room of Angels" are as follows: 1) the Web site Grateful Dead Lyric and Song Finder; and 2) the official Grateful Dead Web site, which is dead.net.

This book is dedicated to my father,
SEBASTIAN MURABITO,
the greatest storyteller I know.

Table of Contents

Berenger (to Jean): Life is an abnormal business.
Jean: On the contrary. Nothing could be more natural, and the proof is
   that people go on living.
   —Eugene Ionesco, *Rhinoceros*

As I walked toward the school I thought to myself that my life had turned
suddenly, and that I might not know exactly how or which way for possibly
a long time. Maybe, in fact, I might never know. It was a thing that happened
to you—I knew that—and it had happened to me in this way.
   —Richard Ford, "Great Falls"

CHASING SAINT GEORGE

That was the summer Cassie got the keys to her dad's trailer by the edge of the field. It was their old Dutchmen, the one Mrs. Kaz swore would sell in a day, the one Mr. Kaz swore no one would ever buy.

He said, "Paula, what do they want with a trailer when they're down here in a family place or staying at Lakeside Cabins?"

She said, "Vacationers have friends, Johnny. One of them is sure to want it."

But he was right. Car after car flew past the blacktop then over the gravel at the end of Shore Road. To us kids, it was where we lived year round. But the fools from Oswego couldn't wait to hit the water, light their barbeques, or pop that first cold one.

"They drive like assholes down here," my dad said.

"Don't say *asshole*, honey, not around the boys. It's bound to ruin them," my mom said.

"Oh, Dottie, they've heard that and a lot worse. It's true. I mean, look at the muck they kick up. Johnny'll never sell that thing if you can't even see it through the dust."

That was the summer I turned thirteen, and Cassie turned brown and got those freckles on her broad cheeks. Her hair was jet black, exactly like her mom's, and her eyes could be either blue or green, exactly like Lake Ontario, which was about two hundred yards behind our houses but off limits because our moms were so afraid that one of us kids would drown. With Mrs. Kaz it was a daily obsession: She came out their front door, looked left long enough to witness two or three white-caps, and then, spotting us on our bikes, her shoulders dropped, and she sighed back through the screened door.

"Your mom thinks we're all gonna drown or get run over by a car," my little brother, Joe, said. "What? Is she mental?"

"I don't know, but my dad says that she's got too much time to think. He says she should get a job over the summer already," Cassie smiled at me. "He says all the other teachers do."

We nodded.

We agreed on everything, us kids, Cassie and her twin brothers, Timmy and Tommy, and me and Joe. Sometimes there were others, Bruce Dryer or the Keegan sisters.

"Come on, guys. Let's go hunt frogs," Timmy said.

And we were off. Always off. Always riding or running to whatever was next.

That was the summer Cassie got her white bathing suit, this two-piece pearly thing that looked like silk. Was I the only one who could see through it? That suit was forever wet, even if we were out in the sun for five hours. Through it, I saw her breasts, two-toned and large and round and always moving. Through it, I saw the rest of her, every crease and fold, all fluid and gleaming like a dream.

That was the summer I got up early every day just to sit in the back yard and wait to hear her voice come over the fence. Maybe she was tired with sleep. Maybe she told one of the twins to share the last of the Cheerios. Maybe she told her mom to stop worrying, that we'd never even think of going to the lake, and so we couldn't drown in it. Maybe it was nothing at all, just the music of their cupboards opening and their spoons rattling. It didn't matter. It was her. It was Cassie Kazinski pouring cereal, and that meant everything was going to start all over again and maybe even be better than it was the day before.

Cassie's mom loved having me over, too. She kept feeding me all of this horrible stuff to eat. Like she put brown sugar in spaghetti sauce and cheddar cheese in meatballs. She made bread with sage in it. Cassie said, "Come on, Mom. I'm only thirteen, but even I know that braised grapes don't go on Spanish rice."

Mrs. Kaz checked her notes and never flinched. "Honey, that's what my experimental recipe calls for. You'll never know unless you try. Now here, try," and she slid a plateful of it in front of Cassie.

Cassie puckered her lips: "I think I'll just have a bologna sandwich today."

She touched me. That's all it took, and I ate her plate, too.

I didn't yet know the whole story behind Mrs. Kaz's odd recipes. At the time, it only seemed to me that she was trying to get one food to taste like two or three different foods at the same time. Weird thing was she taught home ec at the Catholic High School in town. Cassie and her brothers made a lot of excuses and ate a lot of bologna and salami and ham sandwiches, and Mr. Kaz was an ex-alcoholic who chain-smoked Newports and drank coffee all day selling Chevys on Route 104, so his taste buds were shot to hell and back right off the bat. Plus, he studied sales charts, pamphlets, and contracts while he ate, even at our cookouts. He was the only person I knew who could drink a beer without looking at the bottle or eat food without looking at the plate.

One night, I brought home a glowing yellow tuna noodle casserole that Mrs. Kaz made with hot dogs, chopped eggs, and Brussels sprouts.

My father winced at the madness on his fork: "Those priests at Cat

High must not care what the frig she cooks so long as the boys and girls steer clear of each other."

My mom said, "Manny, not around the boys. Let them have their childhood."

Joe and I giggled at our steaming plates, waiting to see if we had to eat it.

Dad swallowed hard, his five-o'clock shadow suddenly glistening. "Good Christ 'til next Tuesday. On second thought, to avoid having to eat this, those kids'll be hiding in the bushes and breeding like rabbits."

"Manny!" Mom shouted. "Now, come on, it can't be that bad. She's an excellent cook. She won that baking contest, and she's written things for the paper. They wouldn't just hire anybody to teach those kids over there." But then she sat to her first slow taste.

We leaned forward.

"I think the woman needs counseling. I mean, I really do. No one in her right mind would do this to good food."

We exploded.

She licked her chops, "Dear Lord, Paula. Is that turmeric?" She took a sip of my dad's Genny Cream, something she never did. Her face wrinkled with alarm, "Manny, I think that *is* turmeric."

We gave the tuna-thing to our dog, a hulking St. Bernard named Saint George, who chose to run away for days at a time but only during the summer.

Once a month, Dad cursed, "That bastard's nothing but a good-goddamned seasonal fugitive."

That one cracked us up, Joe crying tears of joy.

My mom told Dad not to say *bastard*. It might give us the wrong ideas and make us criminals.

If the dog were still loose when Dad came home from work, though, he'd grunt, put on his Yankee cap, and do his futile best to go hunt down the giant.

But on that tuna-thing night, she took another drink from his beer, this one longer, this breath deeper, as if she'd been pulled back from the brink of disaster.

We watched the dog.

The house shook when Saint George took one sniff of the glowing glop, gave us a stare made of august confusion, and then collapsed into a heap on the linoleum floor.

Joe's legs kicked the air.

"That's okay," Dad rubbed the dog's head. "Everybody's got his kryptonite."

Still, I liked Mrs. Kaz. She was sweet, and she was Cassie's mom, and nothing else mattered. So what if she made us hot chocolate in July? So what if she blended anchovies and pineapple juice into her Italian salad dressing? I'd hold my breath and gag it down and smile as Timmy and Tommy rubbed it in and quickly sprinkled powdered sugar on my spaghetti as if it were Romano cheese. I smiled back as she washed dish after dish to re-arm herself with new pots and pans. I heard myself asking for more. It didn't matter. I'd do anything to sit at that kitchen table, look out at our lake, and feel Cassie's sandal slowly come up my leg.

It was a leather sandal.

It was my right leg.

And to keep us from sneaking down to the shoreline, bobbing beyond the waves of her nightmares, and sinking like stones, Mrs. Kaz got us all moving in a wild circle around the inside of their above-ground swimming pool. We created our own current. Then on her count of three, we lay back and let the force carry us around and around and around. One day, I fell back into Cassie, and her hands caught my shoulders, and her legs slid around my stomach, and her feet crossed in my lap.

"You're special," she whispered above the laughs and screams.

Her thighs took in the sides of my body.

We rode the last of the swirl.

Mrs. Kaz stopped to squint at her watch and chirp something about making dinner. Timmy and Tommy looked away, not wanting to encourage her too much, and the other kids followed suit out of sympathy, so no one heard or saw a thing.

Under the water, I reached back and touched Cassie.

She squeezed me once more then swam off.

I knew then, under that sun, that I'd never know a more piercing love.

One day, Cassie begged me to go down to the lake.

"Come on, Charlie," she said. "My mom's chopping turnips, and that'll take her an hour. Look, there's no waves. Let's go in just a little. Only up to our waists. It's so blue today."

"Don't you think we'd have more fun in your pool?"

Her brothers were indoors with my little brother. The Keegan sisters went to Oswego with their mother. The place was sun-baked silence.

She tilted her head, and smiled: "Okay. You wanna go for a spin?"

A few years before, whenever Saint George started running away, we weren't allowed to chase after him for more than ten minutes. We giggled and laughed, traipsed over the fields and across the gravel road, all in bare-feet, never twisting an ankle. Sometimes, I even got to hold Cassie's hand if we had to cross the stream or step over some fallen trees. But it did no good: Always ten yards ahead, the dog stopped, turned, held us in his droopy brown eyes for a second, and then launched off into the marsh before the swamp.

When it was apparent that we'd never catch the dog, and after they added more units at Lakeside Cabins that year and people drove like paradise-bound maniacs once they could see the water, we weren't allowed to chase after him at all if he got loose. Strict orders from all four parents. Everybody knew the dog would go through the last of the pines and maples and then into the greenish black stillness of the swamp. No one could figure out why. Maybe it was the campers and vacationers who called one another to the edge and clapped for the damned thing when he swam out to the glassy onyx middle. We could see his head and hear his heaving breaths, but it was no use to keep calling him. He paddled beyond our pleadings and whatever bribes we could grab, crusts of bread or shreds of bologna.

And sooner or later, there he'd be, collapsed on our front porch, covered with burdock and frog eggs and once chewing on a lake trout that probably got washed into the inlet. My dad would waste ten minutes swearing at the massive animal but end up taking a leash and a bottle of Prell and hauling him off down to the waves. When they got back, Saint George fell on the rug in front of the fireplace, and Dad took a bottle of beer with him to bed.

No, it was no use trying to catch the renegade dog, his stretching orange and white a sprawling over the summer green, and it was no use trying to tell us kids not to chase him. We knew we could get away with it. Mrs. Kaz was the only parent who didn't leave for work, and she was more Doctor Frankenstein in her kitchen than guardian angel in her lawn chair. No, we loved chasing each other in the merry-go-round current of the Kazinski pool, and we loved the sudden chaos of chasing Saint George.

That was the summer Saint George got loose on the 4th of July weekend. The Lakeside Cabins were full, and the beach houses were alive with families and their friends. Mr. Kaz even rented out the Dutchmen for 30 bucks and a case of Genny Cream Ale. We were all going to have a picnic and then take blankets and chairs to the shoreline. From our position in the Bay of Mexico, we could see the fireworks in Oswego, Sackets Harbor, and Alexandria Bay. I wanted to sit by Cassie and hold her hand and watch our lake light up.

I watched the couple move into the Dutchmen. I was jealous. I wanted to marry Cassie and have our honeymoon in there. I pictured sharing a tiny bottle of champagne, like the one my parents bought when we toured the Great Western Winery. A line-worker tossed my mom a cork, and we all clapped. She winked at him. She was beautiful in her rolled up jeans, her red belt, and her white blouse.

My dad gave her a big hug and teased her.

She blushed.

He said, "Nice work, Dot. Next time, wink at the wine maker, and we'll get a bottle of red."

"Yeah," Joe said. "Betcha he doesn't just give out those corks to anybody."

Our tour group was almost into the packaging room when I turned around and saw the same worker toss another cork to a lady in a miniskirt. She was pretty, but not as pretty as my mom. No way.

It was Saturday, about five o'clock. My mom had made potato and macaroni salads, and Dad was wrestling a bag of charcoal. The place was buzzing with flags and parties and music and traffic and barbecues.

Saint George bolted off the side porch, and the usual chase was on through the orchard next door, then the field, then across the stream, then across the road, then into the marsh, then the huge splash into the swamp and the swim out to its center. The swamp was surrounded with people, some in awe and some clapping and cheering and taking pictures. We begged him with our pretzels and corn chips, but as usual, that did no good.

And then it happened.

He didn't get out of the water, shake himself off, and run north.

Saint George doubled-back: He swam to the eastern edge of the swamp and was through the marsh and into the fields again.

"We can cut him off. Come on, let's go," I said.

My dad was calling for us to stop.

Mrs. Kaz screamed, "Johnny, do something!"

By now, there must have been ten of us kids running into the field.

He streaked right by us.

He crossed the road, and we flew after him.

Then the biting of brakes and the screaming of a woman's voice, and the sound—I'll never forget that thudding sound of Timmy going air-born into the branches of a McIntosh tree.

Then the crowd and the men running with ladders and Saint George standing and barking, not letting anyone near the tree.

Dad broke through, jumped on the dog, swore him to the ground, and led him off.

Timmy started to talk. He said his back hurt but that he was okay. Then he asked, "Would somebody please get me down?" And people breathed a little laugh of relief.

A chain of men eased him down.

Mrs. Kaz was on her knees saying the Lord's Prayer and "I knew it, I knew it," all at the same time.

My mom knelt down to hold her.

I don't remember the time passing. But the Kazinskis slid Timmy into their wagon and tore down the road to the hospital in Oswego.

Cassie turned and looked back.

I saw her broad face, her jet-black hair, her green eyes, and then the dust rose up, and I never saw her again.

Mrs. Kaz wouldn't let the family return to the lakeshore. They stayed in Oswego with her parents. The For Sale sign was up in a week.

Word came that Timmy needed an operation, and he'd walk with a limp. But he was going to be okay.

My mom read us the *Palladium Times*. The one doctor said it was a miracle, that if he hadn't hung just right, that if the men didn't take him down just so, he might be paralyzed.

The days followed one another in hot silence.

Bruce Dryer went to the store with his dad.

Mrs. Keegan wouldn't let the sisters out.

Joe swung on the swing set all day.

My mom and dad knew more than I thought they did about me and Cassie. They kept watching me. They took us to the movies. They took us around the Loop in Oswego to Rudy's for fish sandwiches and ice cream. They watched the sunset there. I watched the cars swoosh by.

They whispered things in the front seat.

I heard him say, "He isn't coming around."

I heard her say something about the Baptist Bible Camp up the road from our house.

He shook his head and turned up the radio: "Dot, I've I been called a lot of things in my life, but Baptist will never be one of them."

"Oh, Manny, what's it matter?"

"Huh," he grunted, turning up the song still more.

Joe stood in my doorway one night and started to cry.

"What's wrong?" I asked.

"You're gonna hate me, Charlie."

"Why?"

"Because it was me."

"What was you?"

"I let Saint George out."

"What?"

"I did," his shoulders shook. "I'm sorry."

"But why, Joe? Why?"

"Mrs. Hastings was camping across the street."

"You mean, Mrs. Hastings your First Grade teacher? So?"

"So, I told her all about Saint George in school, and she thought I was making it up, and I wanted to prove to her that Saint George was real. I wanted her to see I wasn't lying."

I stared at the floor.

"Do ya hate me, Char?"

"No," I said. "I don't hate you."

He made me shake on it. Then he came back with his blanket and pillow and slept on the floor by my bed.

I couldn't get to sleep, so after a bit, I woke him up and gave him my bed.

He curled over and spoke to the wall: "Hey, Char, remember that one time Saint George got loose, and those sea gulls came down and were flying all around him, and the people were clapping and going crazy and taking pictures?"

"Yeah," I said. "I remember."

His breathing deepened into sleep.

It had been that last weekend in June when Cassie and I snuck out to the trailer. Our parents were going to a dance at the Blue Trout, only two miles out on the highway.

Mrs. Kaz locked all of their doors and wouldn't leave until Cassie sat on the couch with the telephone in her lap. My mom gave us chips and Coke and told us to go straight to bed after the movie.

Johnny, Paula, Dottie, and Manny left in one car.

Cassie and I had a system worked out. I would hit our kitchen switch twice when Joe was sleeping, and Cassie would answer back with two flashes of their porch light when the twins knocked out.

I agonized until that golden bulb pulsed against the black lake.

Inside the Dutchmen, Cassie lay down on the mattress in her green nightie.

"Give me special kisses," she opened her arms.

I held her close and couldn't stop kissing her throat and neck.

She snapped the band of my pajama bottoms. "We can do it if you want to."

"Do it?"

"Yeah, do it."

I sat up, and she turned me around and eased me back into her arms.

She said, "Or we can just pretend we're in the pool."

"Yeah," I said. "We'll have lots of times to sneak back out here and do it."

We looked up at the ceiling.

She said, "Do you think my mom's crazy?"

"No, I like your mom."

"You're right. She's not crazy, like *crazy* crazy. She just wants to win that teacher's award they've got at Cat High. She almost won two years in a row. But she says the priests will never let a home ec teacher win. Never a gym teacher. Never a home ec teacher. She threw out a bunch of her experimental recipes and then got drunk and cried about it last week. She finally made us hamburgers for lunch the other day. I think my dad is still gonna hide the whiskey, though."

"So, that's why she keeps testing new recipes?"

"Yep," she kissed my ear. "So you can gain ten pounds, and she can be the Cat High Teacher of the Year."

She smiled at me, and I kissed her again.

The moon shifted, and I could see half of her face. We knew it was time to go back. It was after midnight.

I watched her sneak into her house.

Saint George watched me sneak into ours.

The summer ended.

My mom even started stockpiling school supplies.

At dinner that Saturday night, she said someone new was moving in next door, a Mr. and Mrs. Flaunders, and they had two cats named

Salt and Pepper. Mrs. Flaunders had a pottery business and loved the idea of wintering out on the lake.

Dad smiled.

Mom said she couldn't wait to have them over for peach pie and coffee.

They were all happy.

I could hardly breathe.

"Oh," she buttered Joe's bread, "and they finally sold that darned trailer."

"Really?" Dad asked.

"Yep. Paula's father was out this afternoon testing the hitch. He said don't call the cops if somebody drives it away this week."

After a silence, he softly asked, "Did you ask him?"

"No, I didn't," she whispered through her teeth, shooting her eyes from him to me and back to him again.

I looked away.

"He won't tell," she said softly. "Dozens of people have told me that, Manny." Then she whispered, "Paula's orders."

Long after they were all asleep, I got up three times to look at the trailer through our kitchen window. Every time I crept through the living room, Saint George rose up, and every time, there were still more stars in the lake sky behind the Dutchmen.

I woke up before everyone else that Sunday morning.

Saint George followed me to the front door.

I opened it.

The For Sale sign was gone.

Dew glistened on the trailer.

14

Saint George looked at the opened door and then at me. He tilted his head.

I stood in the threshold and opened the door to its hinges, offering him the day, the last of the campers and the vacationers, a few of them up and packing their cars already.

He didn't bolt. He moved past me to sit in the grass at the bottom of the steps.

I sat on the porch swing.

He kept looking back up at me, his brown eyes droopy yet wise in the black mask.

I kept looking out to the lake.

It wasn't ours any more.

My Mother Is a Rosary Lady

I. My Mother Is Darthella, Mistress of Storms

On that first Saturday morning, I came downstairs and saw my father, already showered and shaved, rolling around on the old green couch, laughing hysterically at the TV as Darthella, Mistress of Storms, threatened Kobar the Brave with eternal banishment into the Realm of Endless Doom. Dad gave up his secret: The voice of Darthella was, in fact, my mother. On the screen, the hyper-proportioned villainess stood half-naked, arms extended and fingers producing her famous, raging, neon-pink lightning bolts. At first, I didn't believe him; then, I rushed with great pride as I made out the voice for the first time, and those bolts sent the hulking hero spinning into temporary chaos. *Way to go, Mom*, I thought.

After the cartoon was a hit in the general Pittsburgh area, *Kobar the Brave* got syndicated nationally. But still, nobody knew that the lady who studied drama and music at the otherwise all-male Winston Wilton College up on Polish Hill, the lady who played Olenka in the Glassport Players' presentation of Chekhov's "The Darling," the lady who headed the Rosary Committee at Saint Stanley's church was, in reality, the voice of the hissing, vicious, and savage Mistress of Storms.

"We're saved, Davie boy. We're goddamned saved!" Dad shouted from the kitchen that glorious morning. "The producers are signing your mom on for fifteen more shows, and with her new contract, we'll be able to keep the house! I took the For Sale sign down this morning!"

I was still groggy from my movie date the night before with Roxie Padalecki. We were only fourteen, and our parents let us go to the early showing of *Poltergeist* down at the Portland Theatre about two blocks from her dad's grocery store on Warszawa Street. Roxie with her black hair off one shoulder. Roxie with the worn and figureless Latin cross only inches below the succulence of her throat. It shone there with a dull insistence matching the blunt aching that wouldn't let me go. And Roxie with her old-world refusal to wear perfume: God, every time we were close, I lived in the lustful inhalations of Ivory soap.

"You got your sneakers on, Buddy?" Dad asked, not caring that I was still half-asleep.

I had to run to catch up with him out the door. We went down the hill and over a few blocks to Benny's, where Dad was to buy me my first beer. Like I said, I was only fourteen. Benny shook his head at first, but then served us in the back by the pool table. He solemnly drew closer with two short drafts of Iron City balanced on a faded red Duquesne Beer serving tray. He set it all down carefully, not spilling a drop in his sudden reverence.

"Now, you'll keep this to yourself, Davie—promise." Dad said it quickly, turning to me, all the seriousness of our mission returning like the sweet aftertaste of the beer.

"No sweat, Dad. Not to worry," that last was said casually, confidently, with foam on my lip and a shrug of my shoulders.

Still, he wanted to hear my actual promise, so I became myself again and swore my silence, my allegiance. Dad's eyes sparkled. We toasted even though his glass was already only half full. Then I beat him at 8 Ball.

But he didn't care if he won or not. We were keeping our house, and nothing else could possibly matter.

His attention span for shooting pool weakened into his playful refusal to let Mrs. Stahl leave out the back door until she danced a few steps with him on the checkered tiles.

"Oh, you're too much," she laughed, setting down the two quarts of Stoney's.

Johnny Cash was stuck in prison; my dad and poor Mrs. Stahl spun free. As I ate my fries at the corner table, his joy seeped into me, and I could've danced with him.

I saw in his tanned face that it didn't matter any more how his company had screwed him or the whole town; it didn't matter any more if he'd had his hours cut by nearly a third at the Martin Glass Works, a place where his own father had trained him as a cutter in the plate glass section. I saw that, sure, the world could tweak you off its thumb like some helpless ant hurled into space, but the world could also turn loose this saving craziness that suddenly filled up lives. That was, as long as there were all those unknowable lunatic kids out there in love with Kobar the Brave and his seething Bearcat, Friend of Man.

In a bit, as we were leaving and walking weightlessly back up the alley to Seraphim Street, the world was hitting me somehow, and I thought just for a second that everything imaginable was possible.

II: Cobblestones, Cuff Links, and Upstate Epiphanies

Our neighborhood spilled down from the fenced-in backside of the glass factory halfway up Polish Hill. We lived in simple houses. They were pink, white, yellow, and blue. They were old, but they were well-kept, even beautiful on some days despite being so huddled together and incomprehensibly close to the sidewalks and cobblestone streets. And people loved it up there. My family had lived on West Kolbe Street for three generations.

It was a "poor, depressed neighborhood" when KDKA News came the following Thursday afternoon to interview my dad, a senior foreman at Martin. But it had somehow been sold as a "beautiful neighborhood, exhibiting a rich ethnic heritage" when Winston Wilton College wrote about it in the catalog that had come just days before.

For some reason, that shiny catalog was what my dad was waving into the TV screen as his interview collapsed into anger and frustration. See, this guy Dottsworth from England was supposed to ride in like a white knight to save the day. But Dad and many of his co-workers didn't trust him from the start because he had already "raided" a brewery in Oregon, a canning factory in Alabama, and a shoe company in Maine.

"He's just gonna raid the place. I give him three months to sell it out from under our feet. And there go our pensions! There go our homes! The man wears cuff links, for Christ's sakes! Diamond cuff links! I've seen the diamond cuff links!" Dad yelled like some sort of possessed prophet in gray overalls.

The reporter took two steps backwards and extended the microphone. But Dad was so upset that he couldn't articulate his points about the factory and the neighborhood. He stood there ruby-faced, reduced to two hundred pounds of huffing and grunting outrage. He had gotten beyond language.

"But, Mr. Luzinski, you're a foreman. You mean that it doesn't matter to you or the others that Dottsworth has promised to save the Glass Works?" Knowing his craft, the reporter played the moment well as he kept the microphone in my father's face.

I'll never forget it. Dad stood there, his clean-shaven face glowing pale in the floodlights. He was trying to catch his breath in the thin summer air, staring off all glassy-eyed, the catalog falling to his side as he shook his head. A voice inside of me screamed, "Cut! Cut! Cut! Get his face off of the screen!" But the red light on top of the camera burned bright as a beacon, and we stood there on the street, aching for him.

That night, there he was on our TV.

We silently sat through the story and everything else following it, even the weather and all of the commercials. I don't know what the three of us hoped for—maybe an apology, an explanation, a retraction? I just don't know. But we waited, and nothing else came.

Then, after the *Six O'Clock News* mercifully ended, my parents stood, faced each other, and nodded knowingly. The familiar ritual was now kicked into gear and unstoppable. He bowed, his one hand slowly fanning out in front of him, and he could've been a regally dressed doorman welcoming her down into the luxury hotel of our basement. Her piercing green eyes exploded with impatience as she accepted his invitation, unruffled her summer dress, threw back her shoulders, and became an outraged victim about to take the witness stand at last.

Without a sound, they ceremoniously marched down the warped cellar steps to have at it under the one light bulb in the back, by the dusty shelves of canned Chambersburg peaches.

"I'm sick of you being embarrassed for me. I'm sick of your censoring me," he shouted.

"I've never seen such a lack of faith," she shouted back. "Never!"

In time their words faded, and I heard the flat, constant pounding of each one's slow ascension back up the steps. Dad stormed past me and went down the hall to their bedroom. I heard him on the phone, telling the people at KDKA that he was on medication for stress and that he'd sue them if they showed him again that night at eleven o'clock.

According to the story we all got later, KDKA said that they understood, and they'd certainly pull it from the eleven o'clock broadcast. But there was a slip-up, and they showed it anyway. I'll never forget the look on his face later that night, how he closed his eyes, folded his arms, and sat back exhaling deeply. When my mother flew out the door, her head covered in a kerchief, he didn't even turn to look.

Mom? Well, she was convinced that he had refused to call the TV station. Thing was, she did what she'd always done when she got really upset: She went two blocks away to Saint Stanley's. She was in the back, lighting three blue devotional candles, and saying the rosary.

Her friend Betty Roczinski from the Shop 'n Save store was there with a black eye from her husband, Pete, the alcoholic plumber who washed out of the Pirates' minor league system in the early 70's. Mom and Betty decided to drive with a third woman to upstate New York, to a city on Lake Ontario and a small monastery there, where they were told the Virgin Mary had appeared above the burgeoning pear trees.

When Mom phoned the next day, I could hear the faint chanting in the background, the unbroken litany of the Hail Mary. She refused to talk to Dad. He was staring into deep space, anyway, an empty bottle of Iron City tilting in his lap, his face darkening with stubble. Mom said good-bye and joined the voices before hanging up. It was a Friday. I now know they were praying the Sorrowful Mysteries.

III: Shitty Relief Pitching, Disrupted Rehearsals,
and the Sacred Pear Orchard

A week later, the lay-offs began at Martin, and the owners announced that the workers would only be receiving two-thirds of their pensions. After a closed union meeting that night, a lot of the workers met over at Benny's. People kept telling me how Dad made a great speech that brought down the house. Mrs. Roland, the receptionist at the gift shop there, got down off of her stool, hugged Dad, and called him an angel. She said with his new moustache, he even looked like Robert Redford. The place burst into laughter and applause.

I stayed in the back, watching the Pirates game and shooting pool with Tommy T., who retired from Martin years ago and was losing earthly faith by the second. He cursed the "fuckin' world" with more and more dire conviction as the Phillies came from behind in their half of the ninth.

"Shitty, shitty relief pitching," he said. "Fuckin' world, Davie. It's enough to make a man bust a nut. Oh, you wait, son, until the day you round that corner."

As was the case when Tommy T. got really pissed off, his eyes crossed when he looked at me. This made his nose appear to grow. The ridiculousness of his face against the seriousness of his accusations made me bite back my snickering, and I turned around and stepped out the door.

When I came back inside, someone had pulled the plug on the jukebox, Jerry Lee Lewis's "All Shook Up" grinding to a halt. There was a terrible hush all the way to my bones. I mean, the world shifted. I can't explain it any other way.

Even Tommy T. turned and bowed to the event, his hands in his lap, his lips perfectly still. From the back of the bar, I looked over everyone's shoulders and saw the TV framed and glowing in the darkness of the top shelves. The news broadcast was showing my mother and three other ladies standing in front of Saint Casimir's church, three miles away, on the northern edge of the borough. My father was still bolt upright off his stool. He sat back down slowly, a dark hand coming gently to his left shoulder. Everyone listened. Some people turned their heads to my dad, looked at the screen, and then turned toward him again as if some sort of explanation could be gathered from their double takes.

The reporter came on screen and said, "Bill, at this time, all we know is that the Rosary Ladies have been chanting the meditative prayers in front of Saint Casimir's for about five hours. They were seated inside the church but were then asked to leave due to how loudly they were praying. I have here the pastor of Saint Casimir's, Father Peter Kostka. Father, can you give us your take on all of this?"

The priest blushed, ran a hand through his white hair, and said, "Well, Mindy, the ladies were disrupting a wedding rehearsal. It was the Pavlovich party . . . And . . . well, we did ask them, the ladies, that is, several times to lower their voices, but they refused, it seemed, even to acknowledge us or stop praying long enough to explain themselves. However, one Rosary Lady was nice enough to offer a small gift to the bride-to-be, and another Rosary Lady did manage to compose a note."

"Would you read that note to us, please, Father?"

He fumbled with the folded paper, looked around as if seeking permission, and finally offered: "Well, okay. I don't see why not. It says, 'Holy Mother to visit Saint Casimir's soon.'"

23

"And, Father, it *is* written on some sort of stationery, isn't it?" The reporter leaned in, trying to steal a glance.

"Yes," he held up the crumpled script with its bright blue letterhead. "It says the Order of Divine Mercy. It's in Oswego, New York, which I am told is in the northern part of the state, up there on the shore of Lake Ontario. We're calling them now, trying to reach a spokesperson."

"Otherwise, you haven't taken any official action?"

"We admit we don't quite know what to do, not at this moment, anyway. But we will, uh, have a more official statement and stance as soon as we have more information and can also contact the Bishop."

"Father, our sources tell us that there are parish volunteers frying fish for the ladies in the church basement. Any comment?"

"Ah, no—I haven't heard that, so I have no comment at this time, Mindy." The priest turned and made a bee-line for the church across the street.

"Well, okay, Father Kostka. That was Father Peter Kostka, the pastor of Saint Casimir's church here at the northern edge of Glassport's Polish Hill section, where four Rosary Ladies are evidently *praying* for a vision of the Virgin Mary." Then, as the priest flung open the church doors, the reporter turned to the camera, gave a chuckle of surprise, and closed with, "We will *certainly* have more on this *fascinating* story as it develops, and as we find out *what* is motivating the ladies, *who* they are, and *where* they're from."

IV: Job, Mean Joe Green, and the Unbroken Chanting

Dad and I got into the station wagon and drove. As we got to within a block of Saint Casimir's, the people were either standing on their porches or cautiously descending their front steps and peering toward the Gothic church on the corner. Across the street, patrons filed out of Nancy's Place and then made way for a squat bald man who held a smoldering pipe at arm's length. He scowled, looking like a gargoyle returned to protect the church from the obvious encroachment. In front of Stazinski's Music, some ladies with dangling rosaries stepped from the shadows. I saw a bible tucked under one's heavy arm.

We parked in front of the Paloma Blanca bakery and looked across the street at the four women. We heard the chanting. It was somehow beautiful to me. Still, I wished like anything that I weren't watching it.

"What the hell is this rosary thing, anyway, Davie?" Dad's thick brows knit with frustration. "I mean, you go to Religious Instruction, right? Don't they teach it to you there or something?"

"I don't know . . ." I searched my mind, recalling the Tuesday night classes taught by Father Bill in the basement of Saint Stanley's. I heard the elderly priest's voice booming as he tried his best to reach us kids by exaggerating bible stories. He waved his arms to the "wild stampede" of the Exodus: "You kids today have no idea how fast those Hebrew slaves had to move to haul it out of Egypt!" He made a fist at the "guts and faith" of Job: "You kids listen up, now. I don't care what God threw down at our man, Job. He took it; he took it; he took it. He was tougher than Mean Joe Green!" And he drew back an imaginary slingshot to tell us about the "sharpshooter's aim of the Almighty" when David slew the Goliath: "Kids, you'll never miss your target as long as God is on your side!"

Yes, we were told to pray twice as hard as life was in the first place. We were given lessons in faith, hope, resiliency, and ascension. But I couldn't recall one word about the rosary.

My dad had his hands frozen open in a gesture of emptiness, helplessness, as if my not knowing about the rosary was yet another in a sudden string of incredible tragedies aimed right at him.

"Dad, I'm sorry," I said. "I guess I just don't know."

"Okay," he patted my knee. "That's cool, Davie. It don't really matter now, anyway."

He got out and stood by the car with his arms folded. He lit a cigarette, drawing slowly, buying time, studying the four distant figures.

There was a police car parked, lights off, in the church's side driveway. No one was directly in front of the church; people were respecting that shadowy boundary. I heard one woman in the crowd whisper my dad's name after pointing out my mother. I saw people turn toward him. I saw an older woman holding an unlit cigarette. She leaned forward, squinting toward the ladies, and then shook her head up and down, her mouth opening in the sudden recognition. She turned to her friend and asked: "Betty Roczinski?" They nodded and backed away as if the name were portentous.

Before I knew it, Dad was crossing the street. The onlookers stiffened with tension. The two policemen calmly got out of their car.

"Enough's enough, now, Claire. Come on, let's go home," Dad said, tossing his cigarette.

There was no response.

The cops were closing in on him.

"I say, Claire," he slowed down but took larger steps. "Come on now, honey. It'll be all right. *I did* call KDKA. You can even ask Davie. He's right there in the car."

Again, there were only the four voices, confluent in the single appeal.

The two cops stepped from the curb and cut off Dad's angle of approach. The three of them stood there for a few minutes, talking softly. One officer touched Dad's shoulder. I strained but could only hear muffled voices under the prayers.

Suddenly, Dad lunged. They blocked him off, pushing him back. The mumbling swelled, and the praying got a little louder, too. Dad opened his arms and intensely fanned out his fingers. I thought for sure that he was going to force the moment. But he simply wheeled around. And that's when I saw it. Some of the others later said they saw it, too. My mother looked up and started to move but just as quickly returned her gaze to the statue of the Virgin Mary, which emerged like a figurehead from the corner of the church.

V: Pirogies and Haluski in the Confessionals of Saint Casimir's

The next morning, the Rosary Ladies showed up at Saint Paul's Cathedral in the Oakland section of Pittsburgh. No one was quite sure how they got there. Rumors were that Father Kostka drove them.

The news report we watched that terrible morning said that their steadfast petitions disturbed the early seven-thirty mass. When services had ended, and the ladies had endured the vicious stares of the departing people, the Bishop himself arrived and took charge, telling the ladies that whereas prayer was undoubtedly a good thing, he would have no choice but to have them arrested for disturbing the peace if they did not at least lower their voices.

He allegedly told them, "There is no need to pray so loudly because, my good ladies, the Mother of Sorrows is not hearing-impaired."

In the eyes of many, the Bishop had worked a minor miracle. Especially grateful was the district judge, who was paranoid that the

Rosary Ladies would end up in his court. It came out later that the judge let the Bishop know that it was an election year, and he was in no way going to risk losing the Catholic vote by having to take a legal stand against the ladies. Anyway, although the ladies never broke chant or looked at the red-faced Bishop, they were outside on the magnificent cathedral steps by the time nine o'clock mass began.

The reporter whom KDKA sent to cover the story wasn't as savvy as Mindy Esquerita, and he obviously didn't know how to approach the ladies.

My dad looked like crap. Coffee cup steaming before him, he stiffened and moaned on the couch as if he'd gotten a dose of bad kielbasa.

On the screen, the reporter stretched up the steps and asked the ladies, "Can you tell us anything more today about why you are doing this?"

The two-part rhythm of the supplications never broke.

I began to regard it all as a great poem, a strange, compelling music. I even saw Roxie, all draped in a white robe, whispering the prayers from her full lips.

The reporter referred to his notes, stretched the microphone back up there, and tried again: "How long will you be here? Who has sent you? Uh, will you be breaking for lunch? Is there any truth to the rumor that you ate fried fish and pierogies in the confessionals of Saint Casimir's church last night?"

Again, there was no answer, only the quick *Gloria Patri* and Lord's Prayer before the next decade of Hail Marys.

"Did you *sleep* last night? No one seems to know *where* you went. Can you tell us *who* drove you here from Glassport? What *are* your names?"

I hated the way these reporters put false emphasis on their words. It reminded me of Mrs. Willis stuttering out the lines of poetry to teach us about iambic pentameter.

Then it hit me. This was the same guy who had interviewed my dad about the glass factory. He had lost the waxed moustache, but it was him for sure. Later we learned that he was demoted to the weekend shift.

Dad groaned, "Look at him make an ass of himself. Good. At least those sons of bitches get a taste of their own medicine. God, the damned fools never learn."

We sat there wondering what to do. Dad hoped she'd call again and said he was sure she was coming back home. I felt we should at least go down to Pittsburgh. If we were in the car, driving, moving, doing something—anything—I knew I'd feel better.

Then they cut short the report of a bench-clearing brawl in a baseball game to announce that the brothers from the Order of Divine Mercy, in Oswego, New York, were planning a news release, but first they had to finish praying in the pear grove behind their church. Rumors had it that the pears on one tree were exceptionally large and ripening by the minute. We were, of course, promised film as soon as it became available.

The smirking anchorman also announced that volunteers from the Saint Paul's Altar Rosary Society had agreed to stand protective watch over the ladies, who were still flanked up the stone steps of the church. There apparently was now an argument over whether or not to feed the ladies. We later discovered that the Bishop gave his blessing to meatball sandwiches and cookies but not to coffee or any other caffeinated beverages.

VI: Miraculous Zucchinis, Cistercian Monks, and the Changing World

That Monday night, KDKA began running a news segment called "Looking for Miracles." They claimed to be seeking local proof of the value of the Rosary Ladies' prayers. First, we saw the hairdresser from Butler who was saved from her burning trailer by a parakeet she had trained to say, "God bless you." But once on camera, the frightened bird disappointed its beaming owner by screeching out an imitation of Perry Como doing "It's Impossible."

Next, from South Oakland, we saw the retired fireman who had grown a twenty-one pound zucchini in his tiny garden about two city blocks from the Pitt campus. And there was the zucchini, consuming the screen, big as a watermelon, everything else in the side-yard plot pushed out and misshapen. A tomato was actually forced to grow around a corner. When the man held it up, it looked like a perfect heart. "This is my Sacred Heart tomato," he said. His white moustache dancing as he spoke, the gardener claimed that the size of the zucchini wasn't the miracle. "The miracle," he explained, "is that everybody in the neighborhood knows about it, but nobody has stolen it yet."

When the man said, "yet," his face flushing with expectation, my dad burst out laughing. I thought it was great to see him rolling around on the floor, howling. When he got up, the laughter continued to double him over, and he looked like Quasimodo as he made it to the fridge and back with two Iron Cities.

"What the hell, Davie," he extended a sweating tall-neck. "I give up. Here, have a cold one."

Tuesday night, we watched the news and finally heard the press release from the monastery in upstate New York. It was simple: The

Virgin Mary wanted us to pray for peace, love, and well-being. She had appeared to the Rosary Ladies; she had appeared in Divine Mercy's pear grove; and she would be appearing elsewhere soon. The monk went on to say that the Rosary Ladies had been counseled by a Cistercian monk, a cloistered Trappist hermit who received permission to leave his own monastery and break his vow of silence after having seen the Virgin Mother hovering above the pear trees adjacent to his hut in Kentucky. Brother Michael had then returned to Gethsemani Abbey. He, of course, was denying all requests for interviews.

And that was it. No one knew where the ladies had gone, but they were no longer on the steps of Saint Paul's Cathedral, eating fried fish in its basement, or sleeping in shifts in its confessionals.

Then came phenomenal footage of the pear grove at Divine Mercy. At first, I thought it was ridiculous, but then I sat up and saw it, the one brilliant tree with its colossal golden pears. It was absolutely exquisite. I don't know. I can't describe it. And there was this pinkish-orange light shining down through the branches.

Dad threw up his hands and went upstairs.

The phone rang. It was Roxie. She was calling from her father's store: "If you come around through the alley, I can let you in through the back door." Her voice sounded urgent.

Oh, my God, I thought. *This is it.* Giant pears in Oswego, New York. A magical girlfriend in Glassport, Pennsylvania. No wonder I felt a funny tingling only seconds earlier: My prayers were being answered. Her parents must have stepped out, and with everyone in their houses glued to their TV's, she was calling to me. I saw her lock the front door. We kissed by the dairy coolers, her lips sweeter than United cream. Her cleavage spoke to me above the apron. She led me down the dry goods aisle to the back of the store. Hand in loving hand, we walked down

31

that sturdy cellar staircase. I made love to her in the sweet-smelling hum of the basement. We held one another, nuzzling together by the stacked cases of Furmano's tomatoes.

I drank my beer and kept watching the news for some flash, some update, anything that could be a further sign. I even listened to the viewer responses that played as the credits rolled to the theme music in the background.

There on the screen was my mother's face, her eyes closed, her lips moving gravely. The voices came in: "These women embody all that is so wrong with our culture today. Just put them in jail"; "If it was anybody else doing this, they'd be charged and tried. But no, the Catholics get away with everything."

And then, I heard my dad. Even though he spoke with one hand over the receiver, it was his voice sure as day: "Everyone should leave the Rosary Ladies alone. They're confused. But they're honest. They mean well. Just leave them . . . leave them alone." The theme music swelled before his voice could break completely.

Outside, the sun began to set, and the neighborhood was in that subdued, glowing light where tired brick is resurrected, and faded paint can make its last stand. I wanted to kiss Roxie's face in that light.

"My father thinks you're crazy. He won't let me see you anymore, David. He thinks your mother is nuts for sure, and your father is on the way. He says you'll only inherit it—some theory he read about in *National Geographic*. He's been ranting all day, yelling in Polish, and that scares my mom because when he does that, there's no telling what might happen."

"I thought you said that your mother was the one who was fluent in Polish, but that your father could hardly speak it, that your grandparents forbid it, so he could do better in school?"

"Yes. True. But when he tries, that's when we know he's either really happy or really pissed off. And he's really pissed off. Right after we got here, they argued their way down cellar and all the way back to the furnace. I sat on the stairs and saw her rolling number-ten cans of sauerkraut at him like bowling balls. I was down there all morning mopping up pickles after she missed a few times. We had customers up here walking around like zombies with the three of us up and down those stairs like idiots. I can't take it. I just can't stand it. Now, he's mumbling things behind the meat counter, and Mom's paranoid in the vegetable aisle, telling the pears that they're just ordinary fruit, and overrated at that because you can hardly bake with them!"

Against what I now clearly recognized as the odor of dill pickles, Roxie was telling me all of this at the back door, where it was also clear to me that she wasn't going to let me inside. Her knuckles gone white around the rusty knob, she kept checking over her shoulder as if her mother would attack us with heads of lettuce or clubs of cucumbers. Roxie's words ran together into something I stopped hearing, and I knew that she was dark and beautiful and that I'd never touch her again, and that the world had changed, changed, changed without me. My eyes fell where they had always fallen, and I saw the silver cross disappear when she turned away and shut the door.

I couldn't stand it. I walked around the corner to the front of the store. I wanted to go in there, buy a Coke, shake it up, blast it all over the place, and let him know how crazy I really was. But Mr. Padalecki was showing pork chops to Mrs. Roland from the glass factory, and she thought my dad was an angel who looked like Robert Redford. I wanted her to testify about my family: "These are blessed people, Walter. I'm telling you. They've been touched by the Grace of God! It's *not* craziness. It's spiritual possession. And the boy loves your Roxie. He'll make her life perfect."

How long had they been studying me through the store's ancient front window? They were heads and shoulders and faces above the Heinz soup display. There was Roxie with her broom, her father with his knife, her mother with her white onions ready to go, and Mrs. Roland with her pork chops neatly wrapped in the white paper. I went to the phone booth on the corner and looked in the book.

I flipped and flipped until I got to the S's. All of the Catholic churches. The monasteries. Saint Ursula's Convent. I pumped in the coins and dialed.

I got a Sister Julia. I asked, "What in the hell is this rosary thing, anyway?"

The calm voice said never to swear when discussing holy things. Then she explained it all: the initial prayers, the ten decades, and the fifteen mysteries. But I had already lost her. Her voice was sweet and simple but incomprehensible.

They were still looking at me. Had no time passed at all? I dug for my last bit of change and called home.

My mom answered the phone. I was shocked.

"Hey, Mom. You're home."

"Yeah. Your father's sleeping. So when you get here, be quiet—okay?"

I found out later that the monk from Kentucky had advised the Rosary Ladies to return to their homes, but to await a possible future appearance, perhaps even a national call for Rosary People. She got back home only minutes after I had left.

I was glad, but there in the booth, I didn't know what to say. I wanted to know why she did it, what happened, and if it were really all over. I rambled on and on, telling her about Roxie and sauerkraut cans and pickle juice in the air, and I turned, and they were still there in the window, and I told her that, too, and I might have even started to cry.

She told me to calm down and to come home.

But I could hardly catch my breath, and I blabbed on until the voice of Darthella commanded me to shut the hell up.

I laughed.

"Stay there. I'll be right down to get you."

"No," I said. "Don't. I'm on my way home now."

The operator came on and asked for more money. Slamming down the phone, I left the booth. I made an exaggerated cross in the air, slowly blessing my watchful audience. Mrs. Roland quickly walked away, the meat tucked under her arm like a football. Mrs. Padalecki looked beside herself. She spun Roxie around, and they were gone. Then Mr. Padalecki threw up his arms, looked toward his meat case, and bit out the toothy, wet words as if he were chewing off someone's ear. I don't know where my sweeping blessing came from, but I thought it was the coolest thing I had ever done, so I did it three or four more times to the empty corner, hearing the muted blasts, grunts, and spits of Mr. Padalecki's tortured Polish fade as he receded into the darkness of the distant shelves.

THE STAIN

Le Paradis n'est pas artificial
    but is jagged,
    For a flash,
      for an hour
Then agony
      then an hour
        then agony . . .
    —Ezra Pound
    "Canto 92"

I: I Took My Turn with His Pair of Carpenter Jeans

I took my turn with his pair of carpenter jeans, holding them close and closer still, studying the things as hard as I could with everybody watching me. They all stood there waiting for my guess, and the nervous laughter they hissed when the pants flopped heavily in my hands sounded like air escaping from a tire or a balloon.

I admitted my confusion. I said the stain could've been some cherry pie or strawberry jam, or maybe it was that Cran-Grape stuff Len was always drinking. They nodded, and I wanted to hold us all in that moment, even though it was a moment of not knowing: We hadn't heard anything terrible yet, and we were all still a family in a kitchen, slices of coffee cake still on Mom's special platter, her cigarette smoke a sweetness in the air.

But nobody knew for sure what the dumb stain was. All we did know was that Len's wife, Lizzie, found it in her laundry basket after he'd shipped out for the Gulf that November.

"I don't know, you guys," I said, feeling my arms go slack when I handed the pants back to Lizzie. "Your guess is as good as mine."

Everyone breathed again, moved again.

"I can't even remember him wearin' these things," Lizzie looked at them, and her and my mom went downstairs into the laundry room.

It was nice to hear them joking around as they did the wash together. They were never that close before. Lizzie was three years younger than Len, and she was from Saltsburg same as we were, and well, I guess with Len being so famous locally, you know, to end up playing football at the Naval Academy and everything, hell, with him being smart enough to be only the second kid from Saltsburg High even to get into Annapolis, I guess mom had expected something, I don't know, something more fancy or classy, especially seeing as how much she adored that one girlfriend Len brought home after his first year at the academy, that Michelle. She was the daughter of an American ambassador, and her family had actually been with the president the previous weekend.

I don't know. I wasn't really into girls back then. It almost seemed like another me, some kid in a Pirate cap hiding his *Playboy* under the bed, grabbing a *Sports Illustrated,* and running to sit across the diner table from a woman who spoke four different languages and had spent the last five summers of her life in Europe. I mean, she looked as if she had stepped out of one of my mom's *Red Book* or *McCall's* magazines. Yeah, it seemed like it must've been some other squeaky-voiced kid able to look her in the eye, gulp milk, and say really stupid things like, "Where is Romania, anyway?" and "I'll bet Saltsburg High could take theirs any day in football, huh, Lenny?" Yeah, I said foolish and stupid shit like that and was told to shut up by Len, who was all prim and proper, red-faced, and shaking his buzz-cut head as he spooned more and more sour cream onto his baked potato.

But it was good to hear Mom and Lizzie downstairs laughing and then talking the way people do when they like each other. I couldn't hear the exact words; all that mattered were their voices, the way they gave and took. It was nice, almost musical.

And Dad even went down cellar to fix himself a Scotch at the bar we never used. "Do you girls want a drink?" I heard him ask.

"Sure. But make mine with dinner, Dan," Mom answered.

"Sure. Me, too. Thanks," Lizzie's voice was so sweet that I wished it could've gone on forever.

When Dad came back upstairs, he was laughing, too, clicking his ice and smacking his lips. "That big lug of a brother of yours must've been using his lap as a plate. My guess is grape jelly. What was your guess again?"

I told him I really didn't have a clue.

II: It Lit Up All Soft and Glowing with Blue Oceans

In January, after American and allied bombers flew more than 400 missions against Iraq, and President Bush threatened a troop invasion, we found out that Len would be running raids from the John F. Kennedy. I thought about it and had to admit a funny thing. I couldn't go to school or basketball practice or anywhere else without someone asking me how Len was doing in the Gulf, and the names of those faraway places rang in people's voices: Iraq, Saudi Arabia, Yemen, Kuwait.

I said, "He's great," or "Don't worry. He'll be back in no time." I said things like that, said them as fast as I could. Then one afternoon, the teacher asking me turned and walked away, and the hallway went empty, the lights buzzing overhead.

But the more I dealt with it day after day, the more I finally admitted that I didn't even know where those countries were, so I went to the high-school library and headed back toward the globe, but there were too many of my classmates around, and I felt dumb. I mean, Lenny Pacone was my brother, and he was as smart as they came, man, and I was supposed to be smart, too. I was supposed to know all of that stuff and a whole lot more. Besides, how can you be a senior in high school in 1991 and not know the difference between Jordan, Israel, Kuwait, Iraq, and all the rest of the pieces to that huge puzzle?

So I went to the public library one night after hoops practice. As I walked across the river, I remembered how back when we were little and the bridge was under construction, Mom made Len promise to hold my hand when we crossed it.

The road surface of the bridge was closed to traffic, and the town only opened one covered walkway at a time. It was scary how you could see the Kiski River churning all dark green and fast and powerful down under the steel grid. But when we got there, Len didn't hold my hand because I told him, "People will see me and think I'm a baby."

He understood. But then he got way ahead of me, turned, and yelled back, "Come on, Bobby! Keep movin'! Don't look down! The bridge wouldn't be here if it didn't go to the other side!"

I caught up to him, choked back the urge to extend my hand to him, and stared straight ahead at the swirling snow, knowing it couldn't touch us until we came out on the east side. Still, when the work trucks rumbled past us shaking the bridge, it seemed like my heart stopped beating, and my feet never touched the grating under them.

I thought about those days as I made my way up Point Street to the library. My legs were sore, and I felt that old rush of needing to catch up to Len, and I guess I felt love, too, seeing him slow down, blow into his hands, and zip up his jacket as he waited for me.

I got inside the library and thawed out by one of the old green radiators. The giant portrait of Andrew Carnegie looked down at me, his white beard full and immaculately trimmed, silvery and powerful, his eyes sharp and wise and confident as if he not only knew the location of every city and country in the world but had also been there himself. Hell, how can you ship steel to a place and not know where it is?

I nodded back at him like I always did, like Dad had taught me. "Boys," he said, "if you can look that bastard dead-square in the eyes and nod right back at him, you can just about do anything."

The flustered librarian said, "I'm sorry, but you've only got fifteen minutes." Her voice shook when she explained that KDKA just announced that America was bombing major targets in Iraq.

"Will you be checking out a book?" She lifted her chin and drew a breath.

"No," I said, feeling stupid, confused, and heavy, standing there with all my gear.

"Uh huh," she turned away quickly to some paperwork. She tried to write something, but her pen shook.

Pulling the paper closer, she tried again to write but gave up, looked toward the softly speaking radio in the office, and simply squeezed the pen in her hand. "We'll never, ever learn, will we?" Her eyes went blank.

Back in the corner under the maps of the world, I sat at one of the long wooden tables and turned on the great electric globe. It lit up all soft and glowing with blue oceans and green, tan, and red countries. When I hit the button at the base, it spun slowly, slowly, so slowly that you almost couldn't tell it was moving at all. I sat up and watched it: The Canary Islands and Spain and the Mediterranean Sea and Egypt and the Red Sea and India—all of them inched by.

"I'm very sorry, but we *are* closing early. Could I help you with anything else, then?" The librarian stood composed, suddenly beautiful with the stacks of books behind her.

In the silence she brought, I could hear the overhead lights humming against the soft sound of the globe. I turned off the spin button and held the light switch in my hand. "Well," I lied, "I'm doing this term project in school. And I, uh, need to know what countries border Kuwait."

"Oh, okay, hold on," she grabbed a piece of scrap paper. "Here's Kuwait," she pointed to a tiny green spot I'd totally missed. She wrote down "Saudi Arabia" and "Iraq" and said to come back the next day, that she'd have some books for me if any were left. There was a sudden stillness in her eyes: "Now, of course, everybody and his uncle want to know all about the Middle East. But don't worry. I'll come up with something for you."

The rest of the way home, I kept stopping under the streetlights to unfold the piece of paper. The names of those places were strange and eerie as if they were telling me something, or as if they had some mysterious power, glistening with the flakes of wet snow.

III: Still Some Cloudy Shade of Faded Purple or Faint Pink

In February, when the Navy released Len's name along with six other allied pilots who had gone down and were officially MIA, I quit basketball and stayed up nights thinking about a possible draft. I was going to be eighteen in two weeks, and I was scared.

Dad let Mrs. Baker run the shoe store on Salt Street, and he began watching TV all of the time. He studied every news broadcast he could. When he slept, he left the VCR on Record. After the phone rang off the hook, Mom disconnected it, went into some kind of shell, and didn't speak to anyone. And Lizzie and some of the other support-group wives wrote, called, and constantly tried to get any little piece of information they could. But no one knew anything, or at least no one would say a word.

Dad began to speak in blasts as if he were shouting dire conclusions to the world. Emerging from behind one of his newspapers, he blurted out, "Those bastards always know more than they'll tell. That's why we're in this mess. Manipulation, lies, greed, and oil. That's all it is!"

Then, as quickly as his outbursts were there, they were gone, and the room became ten times quieter. He returned to his scholarship of worldly events, exhausting the local papers and endlessly searching through Brokaw, Rather, Jennings, and CNN.

It was after three o'clock in the morning when I heard the washing machine surge on. Everything about that sound said something strange was happening. I don't know how I knew. I never really had a feeling like that before. But I was certain that everybody in the house had heard it, too, and that everything would be different from that point on. I don't know. I just can't forget it.

In the morning, Lizzie was down there folding all of her laundry, everything except those pants. A few days later, we found out that Mom had washed the white jeans over and over and over that night and then left them there on top of the dryer, where Lizzie was sure to see them when she came by to pick up her wash.

Why'd Mom do it? Was she trying to say that she could take better care of Len than Lizzie could? Was she tired, scared, up at night doing clothes, and she washed them again by mistake? Was it even true in the first place? I mean, maybe Lizzie left them there, or something else? I didn't know. The thing was, the stain was still there, still some cloudy shade of faded purple or faint pink. It was getting harder to tell as I studied and studied them in the yellow light of the basement. I looked around: Lizzie's soap, bleach, and dryer sheets were gone, and I knew she wasn't coming back.

Mom never came with us, but Dad and I went to visit Lizzie out on their farm. It was great up there. As the folding hills leveled out, the snowy woodlands became more distant behind the fields. I even cracked my window and inhaled the fresh smell of the mountaintop above Saltsburg.

Lizzie had dozens of yellow ribbons tied around the branches of the two elm trees out front. It was fun to wrestle with Len's gigantic Newfoundland dog, Yankee, who otherwise sat in his pen, looking out all sweet-faced and sniffing at every car crunching over the gravel road.

We had no idea that it was going to piss off Mom so much, but about the third or fourth time out there, Dad and I stayed for dinner. On the TV, KDKA teased us with an update about Len and the others. But after three commercials, we only got the same old story: His F-16 was found in pieces, and the Iraqis claimed to have captured him and four other American pilots. They were yet again giving the Americans one final deadline to release all Iraqi war prisoners before they began the execution of the downed fliers.

"Jesus Christ," Lizzie said, unable to turn off the set fast enough.

We tried to sit down and eat.

Dad's eyes exploded: "They'd better not torture those boys. That's against the code of the Geneva Convention. They'll have hell to pay if they do." Then he moved his fork around, picking at his ham and sweet potatoes.

I heard Lizzie breathing.

It was on a Sunday when Mom packed some of Len's things in a big box from Dad's store, giving it to us to deliver to Lizzie. I knew damned well that those white jeans were in there, even though Dad told me to look anyway on the ride up the mountain.

Sure enough.

Was Mom trying to apologize to Lizzie, or make her mad, or what?

"Those two have got to work this thing out," Dad said. "For Christ's sake, Lizzie doesn't come over to do her washing. She doesn't even call anymore." Then he paused and yelled, "Well, I can't take it, Bobby. This is it!"

I could see him starting to cry, and I said, "I know, Dad. I know."

"I mean, all this bullshit when your brother is—" his voice broke, and for the first time in my life, watching him gaze out over the hood of the Caprice, I knew what helplessness was.

"I don't need this." He sounded as if he were talking to my mom. "I don't need the clamming up and the washing of those damned pants at all hours. It's a crock of shit, Rose, and you know it is. And Rose, Rosie—"

44

His voice broke again, and he was out of the car by Marshall's general store, slamming the door and shouting something about oil and money and lies. I couldn't hear it all. The wind was ripping apart his words.

A few days later, Lizzie came by with Jody Michaels. Her husband, Tom, was a communications expert in a company that was using something called "smart" cruise missiles. The two of them said they couldn't stay long, that the roads were getting pretty bad, and they had a support-group meeting in Pittsburgh. I don't know if Lizzie planned it on purpose—you know, coming over with somebody else and coming over after Dad had driven to the store. But there was that damned box.

"Lenny will need some of these things you sent over for when he comes home," Lizzie said, her face pale, stripped of all make-up.

"Yeah, especially when he spends the night here or something," Jody managed a smile.

But Mom didn't smile back. After lighting a cigarette, she kept her eyes on the blackened match head.

"Especially the alarm clock. You know what a stickler Len is for getting up early," Lizzie's voice quivered. "Plus, we already have the two alarm clocks now."

Her words hovered there in the hallway like some odd fact that would never change a thing between them even if it had the power to change he entire world.

"Okay, okay." Mom spoke fast as she put down her cigarette, took the box, and walked it to the closet at the end of the hall. I thought she'd come right back. But she didn't. We heard the quiet closing of her bedroom door.

After they left, I looked in the box. There was the alarm clock set for five-thirty. That was sure enough Len. There was a pair of pajamas. There were some underwear, some socks, and a Penn State sweatshirt. And then, at the bottom, folded neatly, there sat his jeans. I unfolded them, and the stain was gone, the one pant leg as good as new.

I couldn't believe it as they hung in front of me. I turned them around again and again. I held them at a distance. Then it hit me that they were actually new pants. I guess it was instinct or something. I don't know. But I put my hands into the pockets and found the crumpled and faded slip of paper that said, INSPECTED BY NO. 7.

That Lizzie. Why'd she do it? She went to all the trouble of going out and buying a new pair of pants, and then she washed them or something but left the inspection slip in the pocket. But why?

I folded the pants again, put them back into the box, and set it in the closet. I turned on the TV and watched a retired Army General moving magnetic pieces across the Iraqi border as he explained how ground forces had to advance despite the new information that captured pilots were being scattered to various locations to act as human shields. I thought about Tom Michaels not coming back. I thought about Jody and saw her crying at Saint Matthew's. I saw crushed cities and dead people in bombed-out streets. I saw the librarian sitting at the globe with her pad and pen, watching the glowing blue ball in its slow, steady, insistent turning. I saw thousands of books surrounding her. I saw the bridge, stark and empty, spanning the dark river that carved through Saltsburg.

The TV rattled on and on, saying things so clearly yet saying nothing. I saw Lizzie alone on the farm, maybe on the day Yankee died with everything going quiet. I saw the yellow ribbons freezing against the trees in the icy wind. I saw Mom in her room lying down with her eyes open, staring at nothing. I saw Dad downtown in his display window, neatly arranging the shiny new shoes but never looking up.

And worst of all, I saw Len, dead and gone, not even a body we'd ever see again, but simply a ghost disappearing a final time into the snowy darkness beyond the bridge. I turned off the TV and walked down the hallway, and it seemed as if I'd always been walking down that hallway, until I got to Mom's door. I held her so tightly, you know, I thought I was going to hurt her. I cried and told her I was sorry that it all happened. And I gave her the inspection slip and told her that we all loved Len so much that nobody knew what to do.

"I know. I know, Bobby," she said, getting up from the bed. She moved to the window and looked out over the white landscape. She lit a cigarette and spoke in a soft, calm voice. I couldn't tell if it were hope or resignation. I only knew that I never heard it before. She said that she'd been staring out at the falling trees and trying to picture the apple and pear blossoms, but that she couldn't.

I told her that they were white, delicate, and kind of star-shaped with five pedals. I don't know. It seemed like such a small thing to say. But I couldn't think of anything else. I didn't know what else to say. That was all I could think of to say.

We sat on the edge of the bed until she finished her cigarette. Then she took the inspection slip and put it in the ashtray, too. She lay back down and closed her eyes.

I took the ashtray out into the kitchen and set it in the sink. I walked down the hallway toward the front door. The house was quiet enough for me to hear the refrigerator kicking on. Or maybe it was the dehumidifier in the basement. I couldn't tell.

I grabbed Len's sweatshirt, went outside, and sat at the picnic table in the cold sun. I stared at the craggy Bartlett tree. I imagined its leaves. They would be dark green. They would be the last to turn. And like the oaks on the ridge, they would be the last to fall.

SOMETHING BIGGER, SOMETHING HEROIC

So they wept, the two of them crying out
to their dear son, both pleading time and again
but they could not shake the fixed resolve of Hector.
No, he waited Achilles, coming on, gigantic in power.
    —Homer
    The Iliad
    22.108-11
    Translated by Robert Fagles

That summer of '73, I was seventeen, and I was a myth—at least in my mind. I mean, I was more than tough and hard and serious and stern. My thoughts were grand, bigger than the port city of Oswego, New York, and, I told myself over and over, *So am I*. Up and running each dark morning at a quarter-to-five, I jogged the three miles down to the misty, slow-moving Oswego River, and I imagined its great history and its unique north-running power as it flowed under the eastern battlements of Fort Ontario and out into Lake Ontario.

I made it back home in time to go to work on the Drunelli muck farm from seven sharp until whenever, six or even later if there were other beds of lettuce to be harvested by the old man's truck lights. But through every ditch dug or irrigation pipe hauled or box of iceberg heaved, my thoughts were beyond any immediate earthly struggle and were on the only thing that could possibly matter in this conquerable world: not simply the sport of wrestling, as timeless and noble as the men performing it in Homer's *Iliad*, which I read and reread at night, but the obsession, the absolute need, to beat Joe MacDonald, a superhuman, kind of full-grown-elm of a teenager, who wrestled in my weight class down river at Fulton High School, and who was working that summer on the nearby Kosavich farm.

Each morning just before eight, the sun warming my bones as I thought of faraway ships poised on the Aegean, the gravity of bronze weaponry, or the brutality of mortal combat, the huge Kosavich Chevys, loaded with laborers, flew over the road that cut through our main fields. As they broke over the hill, I could hear the flatbeds coming like wheeled ships, their gears grinding like the closing of the Scaean Gates of Troy. Then the swoosh of their tires broke against the birdsong.

I refused to look up. Still, I knew he saw me, and that was good: I had been up for hours and was already sweating in my fight to get hard and fast and strong; he was merely a part of some rag-tag gang that lazed into work over the steaming blacktop.

"Good afternoon, ladies," I muttered exactly like my hard-nosed coach did when he was pissed off at us, and I kept on moving, bending, searching out the renegade weeds upon which I had waged war.

"Holy friggin' shit shyola! Did you see the size of the arms on that Joe MacDonald? Angie, hey, Angie? That bull's gonna hang you out to dry, son!" That was Toothy, so-called because in his jigsaw mouth there were mystical expanses announcing bottomless depths.

Although he was forty-two years old and a permanent laborer on a lettuce and onion farm, I still let him get under my skin. But I stayed silent and determined, closing my eyes and straining to recall lines of Homer, lines that would save me and keep me on my mission as I broke ahead of the rest of the crew, head-faking like Dan Gable as I shot takedowns on even the smallest weeds that dared to curl to life around my verdant onions.

"And so . . . muscle is made of protein," Mr. Savona had said to the nodding health science class, a smile coming to his face no doubt because he finally brought us a little piece of the world that we appeared to value.

The rest of my dutiful classmates dispatched this fact to notes they might glance at later. But to me, man, the muscle-protein insight was the stuff of muse-inspired epiphany, and it could only mean that in my unbalanced and unshakable desire to go to Trojan war with Joe MacDonald, I wasn't to eat anything but meat, chicken, or tuna fish. Not only that, but I scorned the carbohydrate-eating softies of this world, people standing aghast at the sweating, insane thing I had become, people like my mom and dad and the rest of my family, balanced folks who knew full well that only disaster awaited an Italian who refused to eat his ziti.

"All right, you guys. Fuckin' time for ice cream." That was Billy Drunelli, calling us from the shade of the Bing cherry trees on one of the most blistering days in July. And that would be Frankie Drunelli, his twin, standing right beside him, handing out the Nutty Buddy bars and such before they all melted. In their mid-fifties, they inherited the old man's strength, and either one could chew his way through a brick wall or set your hair on fire swearing in your face if you screwed up. But they were transformed into children as they carried the silver cooler, laughing it on its way above the stiff green shoots.

As the others took their breaks, though, I stayed out on the unforgiving black soil, the life-sucking yet life-giving muck, and growled through my push-ups, my hands burning into the hot earth. Casually eating ice creams, the shadowy workers regarded me as crazy but hopefully harmless as their ritual of cigarettes, dirty jokes, and pissing into the ditches kicked into gear. A few did imitations of my hellacious face.

"Hey, Angie boy?" Toothy gnawed at his Fudgsicle and yelled. "All's you're doin' is working up a good case of skin cancer, son! Face it: Fulton Joe is God-given. He's gonna chop you up for friggin' kindling."

"Look, fuck," I barked, my face sweat-freckled with muck, "one more crack about Joe MacDonald, and I'll take you out."

Toothy shut up. The rest of the popsiclers were too dizzy with exposure and exhaustion to do anything else but make their little snorts of bit-back laughter and consider me the one who was *really* suffering from exposure and exhaustion. I plodded off with the eternal weed bag restrung around my waist like some piece of ancient burlap war garb.

Then Old Man Drunelli hired a guy named Hercules Gregasos, but no one ever saw him, not even at lunch in the barn. He drove tractors, moved pipe, or disked beds of lettuce after we'd harvested them. He did all of this by himself. Hercules was somehow there and not there, a figure we argued over seeing through the distant heat waves. But in the barn, we gulped well water from cups and jars, and one of the kids from town told the bunch of us another story about Hercules's great strength or his heartbreak or his time in a Syracuse jail, the night he ripped the sink out of the wall when all the cops did was mention his woman's name when they were asking him his side of the bar-fight story.

A legend is here on the muck, on the friggin' muck!

I ate my imported Greek olives and pretended that Johnny from Oswego was part of a new generation telling stories about me, the only wrestler ever to defeat the mighty three-time state champion, Joe MacDonald, and thereby save the city from death, disaster, and the black ships poised beyond the lighthouse.

It was about at that time when my mother threatened to call our school psychologist, Dr. Newton (Figgy, we called him) about my refusal to eat a balanced diet. She blew up the night she caught me putting my slice of bread back into the basket and then rolling the boiled potatoes off my lap and kicking them under my little sister's chair.

"Really, Angelo! And you're a seventeen year-old to boot!" My mom always said "to boot!" either just before or just after she launched into a list.

Yes, she was a list-making woman. In this case, she catalogued the many ways I was making everyone's life miserable. She started with her favorite, "First of all, three clothing items do not a load of laundry make."

She was halfway through her second complaint about my stupid protein drinks when my dad, who had been flipping through the mail, gagged on his toothpick.

"Wait a minute, Connie. Wait a minute."

"What? I'm yelling here. What do you want?"

"You blew sixty dollars on having our family name traced?"

"It was only fifty-nine dollars. It was a special—"

At that, they rose like boxers answering a bell and shifted into dialectical transit, shuffling room to room, arguing the benefits of knowing who we were.

I picked up the booklet that Name History, Inc. had sent. On the cover, Deluca was written in bright gold lettering, and under it were four differently spelled variations. This alone struck me as remarkably scholastic, and I wondered if Iowa State would give me a wrestling scholarship and let me study genealogy.

In the four-page text, it said that our name meant "of the light," that we went back to Italy, back further to Sicily, and that it was even possible that our ancestors were priests or brave leaders in the ancient civilization of Troy.

I was right all along! I am a Trojan!

I could have been Hector transposed through the ages. Sure, our high-school teachers often spoke of Achilles, brave Achilles. But Hector was my hero. After all, he was defending his homeland and his family against the invading demigod Achilles, and Achilles's shield was forged by the god of fire, and at their showdown, Achilles had even more protection from Athena. Why couldn't even our best teachers see that Hector was a mortal man who stood up against the gods themselves? Now that I had proof that I was a Trojan, it was only a matter of time before I became a song on the lips of olive-skinned women, their voices rising in everlasting music.

And just like me, my new girlfriend was tough and hard and serious and stern. Her name was Mel Osborne. I had been going out with Ozzie for about three weeks. It was a drive back into the deep woods of Scriba to pick her up for a date, and my dad hated what those rocky roads did to his Catalina, but I simply couldn't wait to tell her the news.

"And so," I boasted to her mother on their front porch, "it looks like I'm a Trojan."

This meant nothing to her. Putting down her can of Port City, Mrs. Osborne only said, "Yep, old Mel there comes from a long line of Osbornes herself."

Man, I thought, the Osbornes must have had their name researched, too. It would have been better than sex itself to discover on the drive to the movies that Mel Osborne and I were both Trojans. And for all I knew, Mrs. Osborne might have been Priam's wife transposed through time to gaze past me and say that the grass needed cutting.

It turned out that tough, tanned, and gorgeous Mel Osborne was not a transposed daughter of Artemis, goddess of the hunt. No, she wasn't meant for me, my catcher of brook trout and slayer of deer. On the rickety front porch, her white cotton top billowing in the breeze was not an Olympian gown. Her deeply set brown eyes, ringed with the fire of orange eye shadow, were not going to launch every yacht, dinghy, and sailboat in Oswego Harbor. No. No girded horde would need to race over the lakes to rescue her.

"I don't want some hell-bent high-school wrestler, anymore, Angie." She came all the way over to my house to tell me this the following Friday.

"What are you saying?" I asked her.

Instead of answering me, she explained that she had registered for an international poetry class at Oswego State. "Rilke is so beautiful, Angie. Maybe if you came with me, there'd be hope for us. But you've got to give up this wrestling. It's kid's stuff."

You cannot give up your Saturdays!

"But time is running out," I told her, knowing that I had to perfect my single leg takedown with the straw dummy I had hung from the big Cortland tree in my back yard. And then, of course, I had three hours worth of sit-ups to do.

She even gave me back my Uriah Heep albums. She left me for a college sophomore who taught her Spinoza and wrote her love letters in Dutch.

You do not have a single friend in the entire world.

Never mind that practically no one I knew would still speak to me. When the dual meet finally came, the gym was packed with the people of my homeland. The Titanic Leslie West strangled his guitar in the opening of "Mississippi Queen" as the spotlights came on, and the varsity wrestlers hit the mats for warm-ups. I glanced and saw the excited face of Old Man Drunelli. His head rose slightly into that eagle-eyed look of expectation as he inspected us like a field of new onions. But then he smiled and nodded once, conferring upon me the King's blessing to do all-out battle. I heard him call my name, but I never looked up again.

While Mel Osborne became Melanie Marie Osborne, stylized her hair, wore sensible blue eye shadow, and fell in love with Brahms, I had won my first five matches. Likewise, so had Joe MacDonald, setting a sectional record his last time out by pinning a wrestler from Mexico High School in 10 seconds. My stomach churned during every bout before ours.

Fulton was an excellent team, maybe the best upstate New York had ever seen, and they were slaughtering us, destroying our walls, capturing and enslaving our women, and raiding our treasure troves of art. My people fell by Pazzuska's Bakery on Bridge Street; they were hamstrung in front of City Hall on West First. Two bouts to go, and I was up and stretching. I swore I wouldn't look, but I did.

That is him, coming on, massive in red.

When the whistle blew, Joe MacDonald stared at me with a dull wisdom that was glossed over with a friendly ignorance. His shaved head was nearly square; his squinting eyes were closely set, but they opened to green beams of purpose.

My coach said, "Damn, Angie! That boy's family tree is missing a few branches."

Perhaps that was true, but he possessed the speed of Achilles.

You are tough, strong, and fast. Shoot!

I shot my single leg over and over again only to smash my head into his stone knees. No yielding, straw-filled dummy swinging from a fragrant tree. Most wrestlers sprawl when under attack, but not Joe MacDonald. He stood straight, pushed me off, and made me look foolish.

Then as he moved back, I shot an ankle pick that would've toppled any other human being. But Joe MacDonald was not subject to the rules of gravity. His thigh was made of granite, and stars burst inside my skull.

This fuck is a tree come to life!

Did I get up each cold morning for nothing? Did I give up Milano's bread for no good reason? Did I absorb Homer's *Iliad* into my blood on a whim?

In a split second, I was down, and as he chucked me like a box of lettuce out of bounds, he said, "Hey, Deluca, I heard you said a few things about me."

Now, the people, *my* people, those whom I defended, laughed, laughed me all the way back to a toothless farmhand eating ice cream in the shade.

Joe MacDonald head-butted me square in the ribs, and I buckled. The referee blew his whistle and waved back both benches. I can only remember my fist flying into his forehead and the utter numbness that shot up my right arm. The crowd sighed. Everything froze. I heard the ancient Aegean wind swirling through my headgear.

His arms opened as if he were preparing to catch yet another box of iceberg from the rollers inside a refrigerated trailer. Then his whole face opened widely, as if it were now seeing the world for the first time. And then, just as quickly, it shut like a great book.

He collapsed with a thud like the Cortland dummy when its strings finally snapped. In the few seconds that it took this to happen, my ribs caught fire, and I knew I broke my hand, but I burned with the rush of absolute victory.

Now, both benches did clear, and I shouted, "Asshole, asshole, weed-head, Achilles!"

But the Fulton heavyweight unloaded on me, and my last memory was of a world collapsing from the epic to a series of white-hot explosions and the taste of my own blood.

You'd have thought I set the school on fire the way my mom and dad and Father Quatorzzi and Dr. Newton all gathered the next night at our house and circled, circled, circled me, slowly, studiously, and finally sadly like the last mourners to whisper the name of their fallen hero.

They eyed one another, determining who was going to speak first. Figgy inched closer to me. He sat, folded his arms, and took a deep, concerned breath.

"So, Angelo, you've been kicking your mother's baked potatoes over to little sister's place at table?"

He wore that look he always got when he had found the complex-yet-simple underlying psychological explanation to one of our teenage misadventures.

I am not their hero.

"He's been doing it now, months on end, Doctor," my mother smacked her lips around the complaint.

"Is this the case, then?" Figgy asked me.

I am not their hero.

"I'm afraid so, Doctor," my dad concluded.

I am no one's hero.

Dr. Newton nodded at my mom, who nodded at my dad, who nodded at Father Quatorzzi. Instinctively, Father Quatorzzi turned to nod to me, but I dropped my head, refusing to look at him.

"Exactly how long have you been out of whack like this, Angelo?" Figgy opened his hands to catch my answer. "How long have you been neglecting your proper eating habits, your mother's pasta, her good vegetables? We're told that you either starve yourself or else eat only can after can of tuna. How long can a growing boy remain rational eating canned fish alone, I'd like to know? All of this, and," his voice dropped tragically, "and yet they discover a box of Slim Jims under your bed?" He took a Slim Jim out of his coat pocket and waved it like courtroom evidence. My sister smiled her get-even smile, and I knew that she must have passed out the little sausages like party favors.

Piercing the lull, my mom began a list of told-you-so's primarily aimed at my dad, who taught me how to wrestle in the first place. They took a brief, two-room argumentative tour, apparently remembered that we had company, and returned to sit down and look satisfied that they had done their part.

My mom whispered to Father Quatorzzi. She sounded hurt, and I loved her a lot just then. They were waiting for me to speak. But how could I tell them of the fall of my Troy? How could I express the detonation in my soul? No. It wasn't about pasta or tuna or vegetables or bread. It wasn't about cold potatoes on the green tiled floor. It was something bigger, something heroic.

And in my hardness, my mind refusing to accept the defeat by default, I didn't like Figgy's familiarity, the way he so compassionately theorized about the chemical imbalances within my brain and the ease with which the world could be set right.

"Angie," he handed me the Slim Jim, "it wouldn't kill you to eat a real piece of sausage, too, or a slice of Asiago and a hunk of bread. What? A little salad? For Christ's sake, kiddo, you're an Italian, so eat like one!"

They began laughing in the kitchen, the smells of coffee and cigarette smoke blossoming. Father Quatorzzi turned back to me, engulfed my hand in his gentility, but then scooted to join the others when my mom called everyone out for brownies.

I heard myself promise never to hit another wrestler again and to write my apology to Joe MacDonald and his coach as soon as my hand healed. The words echoed behind me up the staircase, and before I knew it, I was on my knees trying to pray. But I didn't know exactly for what or to whom I should pray. Should I pray to Father Quatorzzi's God, or to the spirits of ancient warriors who knew what I had gone through as they moved in their eternal grace high on Olympus? I stayed there until my knees ached with not knowing, until my right hand stopped pulsing, until I accepted defeat a bitter drop at a time, until I ran out of poetry, curled on the carpet, and fell asleep.

Katarina Sistellinos and Big Dave Bates

And all that's best of dark and bright
Meet in her aspect and her eyes . . .
    —Lord Byron
    "She Walks in Beauty"

I: I Knew I Looked Like Charles Laughton in *Saint Martin's Lane*

I couldn't help but overhear Katarina Sistellinos and her boyfriend (are you ready for this one?), *Hank Williams*, going at it on the other side of that thin apartment wall. They hadn't missed a noisy night in the Pittsburgh August that they had been in the building. I almost pirouetted that fist time I saw her, the box of cooking utensils pushing her caramel breasts to the sky. She seemed more a holy mystery than a woman.

I heard them with bizarre clarity, the late news flashing on the little black-and-white screen and becoming a social riddle that no one could answer. I promised myself that this time, I would not, this time, I must not. But more out of disbelief than fascination, I gave in and tilted to the wall, listening hard through the swelter for *his* noises.

You see, that was the point: Inevitably, there were none. Again and again, it was Hank Williams going like some sort of perfectly oiled machine, and Katarina, the impeccably dressed junior executive, making such hideous grunts and growls that a wild boar was pausing somewhere by its bush, perking up its head, and giving an intrigued stare into the jungle.

So, okay, I coveted the kind of woman who did all of her shopping at Kaufmann's, and I happened to watch a few too many nature shows on PBS. I know full well most of my downfalls, and my TV set struggles with what little it can get. Excuse me a moment while I massage the feeling back into my right ear. There.

I knew that I was getting rounder in those days and that I looked like Charles Laughton in *Saint Martin's Lane*. A few of us sat out at the bar and watched the classic film after the kitchen closed a few days before, and Bernice, the head waitress, paid me the odd compliment. I'm sure she thought she was being sweet, and really, she was. I mean, she looked up at the big screen when Laughton was giving a great speech, did a double take at me, and then astonished respect flooded her face: "My goodness, Louis. Now that I think about it, the physical resemblance is quite striking." She said things like "physical resemblance" and "quite striking" because she admired that I had at least tried to go to college. The bunch of us toasted my temporary fame, the film pressed forward, and so did our makeshift party.

Yes, I knew I looked like Charles Laughton, and I knew that I was only a dishwasher with a halfway-decent joke now and then for Mrs. Ruggio and Margie while they made the ravioli or gnocchi in the kitchen. I knew I survived three years at Pitt and then quit twenty-one hours shy of my degree in philosophy, and I knew that all of my friends who were in graduate schools or else had careers already blinked kindly at me when I told them that one day I would have my own little Italian place with checkered table cloths and straw-covered bottles of Chianti— the works. I knew all of that, but still, for quite a while there, I thought I knew a little bit about women, love, and life. See, I even developed this theory.

63

Not long ago, I had this girlfriend Debbie (okay, hang on for this one, too), *Debbie Reynolds*. She was a wild one. She was from Montana, and the first time I met her, she said that she had to go back out there because she had a chance to train in the rodeo, or something like that. I don't know. She was distracted, and she spoke so fast that she was hard to follow. With her, I more or less held on for the ride. I mean, I never saw her on a horse or anything like that, and maybe she was crazy like Mrs. Ruggio said on the night Debbie wouldn't eat both of her meatballs, and Mrs. Ruggio, the mother of those meatballs, stood there with her arms crossed, simply unable to process the disrespect.

"I don't know what she is, Louis," Mrs. Ruggio shook her head when I brought back our dishes, "but she's no rodeo rider in my circus. They've been here before. Those people clean their plates!" With that, she blessed herself, scraped the uneaten meatball down the disposal, flipped the switch, and huffed back to her pizza oven. You had to love Mrs. Ruggio.

Pittsburgh's a huge city, I told myself as I walked back out to the dining room, and suddenly the first part of my theory was born when I slid into the booth across from Debbie: *Our lovers came from everywhere, so you couldn't expect them all to like meatballs, and, logically speaking, there had to be rodeo riders where you least expected them to be.*

Anyway, Debbie was small and lean, and I was a little lighter then, too. Well, long story short, she liked to put on her pink and black cowgirl hat and then tie me down. There, I said it. Once or twice, as foreplay, she chased me around and lassoed me. Well, okay, not just once or twice, and I admit that after a while, it got to be my own idea, but still, I figured that Debbie's whole nature was fast and fierce, and so she'd appreciate being in control. Plus, there was the whole thing about growing up out west. So, she liked to tie my hands once in a while? She was always gentle about it. It became understandable to me. And then, tethered to the bedposts, I saw the second part of my theory: *Because love is giving, lovers give lovers what lovers need, and so what if you've got to go through several packages of nylon rope along the way?*

"Come on, baby," she said to me. "Let me tie you down, and then I'll make you some of that Eye-talian food you like so much."

I mean, who could resist such a seduction? She enjoyed half hitches and cow hitches and sheepshanks so much, who was I to kick up a fuss? True happiness is fleeting, and you do what it takes, wrist burns or no. Besides, my hands ached so much from doing dishes all night that I liked them perfectly still for a while. She was even nice enough to lotion them and make any necessary adjustments to the knots. Okay, while she had me there, she may have whipped me and called me a "worthless little doggie," and she may have said something about riding the human rodeo. But that's all beside the point because that's when the third part of my theory came into view: *Lovers say and do stupid things because they are caught in the swirling magic of love, so lovers should never hold lovers too accountable.*

The point was that even though she rode me harder each time, and even though she said something about her other boyfriends being better horsies, her auburn hair flapped like wings ascending, and her tiny gold bronco-buster earrings dangled down, and her face contorted as she let out her victorious hoots and yips, and there eventually came a point of extreme softness, release, and giving. She lowered her head, joining me in deepest concentration, and she gave herself to me. She was rough in the saddle, but Debbie Reynolds had beautiful orgasms. Of course, I never noticed this until it was too late. And so, at the bar one night, the fourth part of my theory washed ashore: *There weren't enough orgasms*

65

to go around in this life, so lovers needed to help out lovers as much as possible, and if a little rough-riding was what it took, well, then, so be it.

This brings me back to Katarina Sistellinos and Hank Williams. About the tenth time I overheard them, the fifth and most crucial part of my theory snarled at me through the wall: *If there were such a wide variety of lovers and such a wide variety of orgasms, then there was an "orgasm continuum," and the orgasm continuum ranged from beautiful (soft, giving, and releasing) to hideous (loud, growling, and absorbing).*

"Hey, Louis! I need that scaloppine pan, pronto!" Chef Paulie called to me one night during dinner rush and a banquet.

"Hey, Louis! I'm runnin' too low on coffee cups out there. Don't bust my balls. Just get me a fresh rack!" Bernice was right behind him.

Scaloppine pans, coffee cups, and busted balls? Hey, how could they bother me with such mundane things when I had my "orgasm continuum" debate to settle? I mean, if they were orgasms, then they were good, and if they were good, then at least in part, they were beautiful. The rest of it was up to the particular individual—you know, how one personalized his or her orgasms, sort of signed them. So whereas at first hideous didn't seem to be the right word for the far end of the continuum, the more I sat there and listened to the grotesque noises coming from that gorgeous Greek woman, the more I became convinced that *hideous* simply had to be the correct word.

And then—you guessed it: The sixth part of my theory screamed into my brain with a passing Pittsburgh ambulance: *Orgasms were part of love, and if love defied all logic, then orgasms must defy all logic, too. They could, indeed, be both beautiful and hideous at the same time.*

I was so blinded by that latest theoretical breakthrough that I got myself an ice-cold can of Iron City and toasted the orgasmers and orgasmees of this mortal coil (present company, of course, excluded). However, even though my work had brought me enlightenment, I still wasn't happy. Day after day and night after night, as I polished silverware, restacked spaghetti bowls, or ran the dinner plates through for a second cycle, I told myself, "Hey, Lou, let it go. Get ear plugs or something. But let it go. You've got to quit obsessing about this beautiful-hideous thing, this orgasm-continuum thing. You'll find a woman one day, and then all of this theorizing will end in happy practice. Mrs. Ruggio's niece, Gina, she likes you. Besides, you only want Katarina because you can't have her."

And amazingly, the voice in my head turned into the voice of Morty, the Jewish fruit and vegetable guy who delivered to the restaurant.

"I need spaget side dishes, honey," Alice said. "Let's get on it, Louis."

"What?" Morty was saying inside my head. "Nice Alice there, she needs her spaghetti side dishes. Well, spaghetti side dishes she'll get. Twenty I got right here. And nice ones, too."

And then—you guessed it again: The seventh part of my theory was born in Alice's smile: *We all had something to say about love, so life made more sense when we listened to everybody, even the produce peddlers inside our heads.*

Then Morty did what he always did. First he said, "What? Life is unknowable. That's the only theory. Any more, and you'll damage your head." Then he grabbed a plate and some silverware and said, "Here, Louis, sit down. These tomatoes are from Westmoreland County. The best. I'll slice us some. Put some bread and butter, and it don't get no better."

Then something happened during the nights of Katarina's and Hank's riotous love making. It was so traumatic that I couldn't even conjure up Morty's voice anymore. No more comical one-liners on tomatoes with bread and butter to take the place of paradisiacal sex. It hit me: These were simply ordinary Tuesday or Wednesday nights, my nights off most of the time, and yet Katarina and Hank had somehow found ways to celebrate each one as if it were a holiday. They had discovered heaven; I had theorized myself into hell.

Then something really perplexing happened. Hank began to make noises, little soft whisperings like, "I love you, baby," and things of that nature. And Katarina stopped growling and hissing and started sighing like summer breezes. She even started singing to him in Greek. And damn if he didn't start singing back to her, exactly like the real Hank Williams himself. They had found a way to serenade life in apartment 3A.

These developments shattered my love theories to such pieces that I had no choice but to leave and start walking, just walking, step on step on step. I walked up Fifth Avenue. I walked past Pitt's Cathedral of Learning. I walked by Carnegie Hall. I walked clear over to Schenley Park. I walked up its huge hill and finally sat on the lone bench at the top and looked back at Oakland far below me. I could see my building. I could see its steps, its stairs, and our apartment doors. I could see that woman, her breasts beautiful when at last they stopped heaving. And I could hear her song: Oh, it was beyond words, sweeter than the delicacy she made you close your eyes to receive.

II: On the 54C and Thinking of Horace Walpole

I knew it was Saturday night and that my pay envelope bulged in my front pocket. I knew Gina Ruggio invited me to a party, invited me the night before in front of her aunt at the restaurant, and that I had said, "Sure. I'll meet you there."

I knew that instead of meeting all of her Pitt Pharmacy friends, I was taking the 54C downtown, where I would again hire the fiery, olive-skinned woman named (get ready for this) *Donna Reed* to snarl loudly and then hold me gently and then sing softly in her best make-believe Greek (for which she charged slightly extra). And I knew that I really felt something for her but would never even tell her my name. I knew it all. Nothing slipped by me with my silver flask of Jack Daniels and my pocket English-Greek dictionary, which Donna refused to use.

"It's unprofessional," she told me last time. Then she turned off the light and launched into her poetic gibberish.

And I knew that I was on my way home now, laughing hard as I stood at the bus stop, this quote by a guy named Horace Walpole (no kidding on that name, either) shooting into my head as Hank Williams crooned "I'm So Lonesome I Could Cry" from a boom box being hugged by some poor kid stoned out of his mind. Walpole said that life was a comedy for those who thought and a tragedy for those who felt. I mean, I couldn't believe the timing of it all: Walpole's voice, Hank's sorrow, and the utter desperation on that kid's face, like someone was going to steal his boom box or even worse ask him to turn it down.

So I imagined old Horace on the bus next to me, hitting my flask and insisting that I take him seriously, that I think, think, *think* the absurd heartbreak of life, think it into my veins and conquer it there.

And so, I obliged him, offered him a sip, and laughed, laughed until the woman across from me held her purse even more tightly than the kid now behind us still clutched his boom box.

III: She Wept Like Vivian Leigh in *Saint Martin's Lane*

After my shift that next Monday night, I sat at the bar with a few regulars. There was Johnny and Francis and Mr. V. nursing his Crown Royal and ginger. And there was Lindy Bonacorsi. He used to box a little Golden Gloves back in the day. Lindy had good cigars and better stories, but even he turned the floor over to Jo Jo Mancuso, the owner's grandson, who told the best ones of all because they were the stuff of lost legend. You see, his grandfather, Big Dave Mancuso, fought in illegal, back-alley bare-knuckle brawls.

In his white shirt, black tie, and red vest, Jo Jo was a methodical sipper of Wild Turkey, so it took a while for him to launch into one of the stories. I'd worked there for three years and had heard as many versions of some of them. They were never requested; they grew out of the air. They were told only when the women, who hated them, were not around. They were, in short, well worth the wait. And sure enough, somewhere into his third bourbon, Jo Jo tossed some more ice in his glass and got into his stance, fists up, his back foot hitting a case of Iron City empties.

In his utterly singular identity, David Bruno Mancuso, the brown-eyed man with the twisted nose and eternal grin, was resurrected in curling blue smoke and raised glasses. From where I sat, I could see into the main dining room, where a portrait of Big Dave and his beautiful wife, Nunzia, hung above the oldest booth in the place, a booth that had seen the likes of Frank Sinatra, Joe Frazier, and President Bill Clinton.

Against shots of Wild Turkey all around, we heard the one about Big Dave and Long John Withers of Philadelphia, a towering man who could punch like a mule but who had no jaw. Big Dave's life was blessed. It had no small moments. With Jo Jo feinting by the beer taps, there was hardly a move that failed, rarely a combination that wasn't deadly. There may have been only nine or ten fights that people told of, but not one telling had him losing. Sure, he suffered busted ribs, broken hands, and a ruptured spleen, but he also knew true success, true love, and he had an uppercut from the gates of hell.

Another Wild Turkey, courtesy of Lindy, who liked that I enjoyed cigars, and I let Jo Jo's constant narration up and down the bar become *my* story: As he turned in front of me, he told the tale of *my* bare-knuckled fists, *my* iron jaw. The name wasn't Mancuso; it was Bates, Big Dave Bates. The year was 1939. Germany invaded Poland. The World's Fair was in New York. And you couldn't come into a Pittsburgh back-alley unless you had money for the purse and money to bet. I moved in the dim light where there was neither judge nor referee nor timekeeper. For the massive auto worker and his friends from Detroit, the alley between Meyran and Semple closed in, became a perfection of brick and stone and howling.

As Jo Jo got to the part about Nunzia's bitter disgust after each fight, I pictured coming home to the cool sheets and to my Katarina.

"I will not speak to you, David," she bit through every word. "You fight like an animal in the alleys." She stood and turned away from me.

But since it was heaven, she turned back around and gently reached for my swollen eye. She fell to me and wept like Vivian Leigh in *Saint Martin's Lane*.

71

She said, "David." She breathed, "Dave." Then she kissed me and whispered, "Davie . . . please."

She soothed my blackened brow with cold towels, rubbed my body with alcohol, bandaged me. And as brutal as I was, her love made me beautiful, calling me back to the flesh as her whispers melted to sighs that became the music of our souls.

IV: Just This Side of the Wine Cellar

In the dark of the restaurant basement, even colder now with the first snow outside, I took my break and did jumping jacks, my counting system tied to the cases of Three Sisters's minestrone soup. This was the ancient concrete floor of my life. This was the dank smell Pig Iron Pete inhaled when he could no longer focus.

"Louis? For Christ's sake, honey. Where the hell did ya go? I need those platters for the seafood specials out there." Bernice called to me from the top of the stairs, but with her bad knee, she'd never take a step, never hear me doing my sit-ups, never know I had two more minutes left to push Chicago's Tommy McClelland up against the stone wall just this side of the wine cellar.

V: Sinning in the Name of Heartbreak

Mrs. Ruggio was the only one to notice that I had lost weight. Even though she refused to speak to me because I stood-up Gina, she began feeding me when I least expected it. It started with two midmorning sfogliatelle silently placed before me like sugared oysters. Next, when I refused to eat with the others before the shift, she delivered a dish of homemade gnocchi, her thick hands surrounding the sudden bowl. "Eat," she sighed with equal amounts of gravity and hope.

Then she stood before me one night, her eyes filled with equal amounts of disappointment and compassion. "Here," she said. "Take a break. Have a little fettuccine and sausage. It's the hot like you like."

My head spun. Her stained kitchen whites were radiant in the garish fluorescent light. She handed me the hideous thing of beauty and walked away.

After she left for the night, I sent the food down the disposal. Had she seen me do it, she'd have prayed the rosary twice and then demanded that I admit myself eight blocks up at Western Psychiatric for therapy of the first order. I mean, the sausage was her own homemade. And the sauce? Well, sauce was salvation itself. To throw it away was to turn your back to God. And thus, my stomach ached with the final part of my theory of love: *At times, you needed to sin in the name of heartbreak just as you needed to sin in the name of pure love. This was because they were the same thing.*

VI: I'll Be Valentina for You

I wasted my whole day off chasing information on Pittsburgh's illegal back-alley, bare-knuckle brawlers of the thirties and forties. Nothing. No one heard of such a thing. Not even the slightly bemused sportswriter who gave me half a minute at the *Post-Gazette*.

Oh, the face of the Pitt librarian who recognized me from the old days.

She said, "I'm sorry, Louis. But there doesn't appear to be anything on that topic in our databases. However, I'll keep looking if you'd like."

"No," I said. "That's all right."

73

I knew that she thought, *How on earth do you go from researching Jean-Paul Sartre to illegal, back-alley bare-knuckle brawlers?*

I almost told her that my near-degree in philosophy had prepared me well for these real-world dilemmas. But instead, I bummed a quarter from her and caught the bus downtown.

Back in Oakland, the wind cutting me to the bone as I walked home, I admitted that I was not a back-alley bare-knuckle brawler. I was nothing more than a freezing dishwasher with wet shoes and a torn bus transfer. I didn't know how it all started. I simply didn't know.

I never should have left college, never should have listened to Katarina and Hank, never should have let the rodeo rider get to me, never should have stood-up Gina Ruggio when all she wanted to do was take me to a party and cheer me up and maybe meet me once in a while at the restaurant for a cannoli and coffee. I never should have stopped living my own life and theorizing everything else into snowy slush.

My head was down, and so I didn't see her in the lobby of my building. She was the last person I could have faced at that moment. It was Donna Reed, the woman from downtown Pittsburgh. I hadn't seen her in three weeks. In the half-light, she didn't look so long-legged, olive-skinned, or sexual. She sat on the steps, hugging the knees of her jeans, a small traveling bag tucked between her and the railing. Speechless, I blew into my hands and tried to buy every second I could.

In fragments that echoed through me, she said that two very serious men were after her because they thought she had stolen four grams of their cocaine.

"I don't even do that stuff," she looked me square in the eye.

She said that she needed a place to stay, even if only for a few days, that she trusted me because I was a thinker, and that she could tell I was sensitive.

"I had a friend take me to Shadyside, you know, to this exact place where I used to live. But then I doubled back, through back yards and everything. What I mean is that no one knows I'm here. I swear."

I stared at her water-logged boots while she said she was certain this was the right place because I had written it down for her myself and told her to visit sometime. I guess I even said that I was a chef and that I'd cook for her.

"But your neighbor, the guy down the hall, he said that he'd never heard of like a Big Dave Bates. He said there was a regular Lou Bates in 3B, though."

"Okay," I finally said, sitting down next to her.

"Please," she whispered, her head turned away, "just for a few days. I'll do whatever you want. I'll be whoever you want."

I was certain that I had died, maybe moments before on icy Meyran. Or maybe I had been dead for months now, losing my soul on that drunken night when I told her my name was Big Dave Bates, and that I was a bare-knuckle fighter. Maybe she was somehow sent by God, had been sent all along to make me reckon for what I'd done. When the light outside shifted, the foyer mailboxes ignited, and the side of her face turned gold. My neck pincushioned with sweat.

"I'll be Valentina for you, like every night I'm here," she promised. "I didn't steal Ricky's coke. That shit makes me puke."

"I know. I know," I said. "Can you do one thing for me?"

"Sure."

"Stop being so scared. Okay?"

"Sure, okay."

I wanted to take it all back, to tell her I'd never ask her to play make-believe Greek singer again. I wanted to release words I didn't even know.

We walked up to my door.

"Who is Valentina, anyway?"

"Sorry," she said. "Katarina, right?" She smiled playfully.

I breathed in the reprieve I'd been given.

Her eye make-up ran, and I gave her a tissue once we got inside.

She was completely beautiful.

"I'm really sorry, Lou."

"That's okay. I'm the one who's so stupid."

"I've got a sister up in Erie. I guess I could—"

"Don't worry about that. Stay as long as you'd like. My name never was Big Dave Bates. That was like a joke I played. I guess it was on myself. And I'm no bare-knuckle fighter. I'm a dishwasher about three blocks from here, down at Mancuso's restaurant over on Bouquet. Look, they're still serving lunches now. Let's go over there and get something to eat. Mrs. Ruggio's wedding soup maybe."

She threw down her bag, blessing the hardwood floor.

As Donna and I left the building, Katarina Sistellinos stepped out of a cab and danced through the slush to the front steps, her red leather coat flying open below the knee, and the white flecks on the back of her dress blurring by like snow out a bus window. For the first time since I had known her, I did not turn my head. I had no theoretical explanation, and that was fine by me.

Donna and I pushed toward the restaurant. When cars passed by, she turned her head away, and I promised myself that I would protect her for as long as I could. I told her about the restaurant, about the regulars, about Jo Jo, and about the *real* Big Dave Mancuso. Her face lit up with the kind of curiosity I had expected from the librarians and newspaper people of this world. She listened intently, and for a moment, I couldn't tell if I were making sense or babbling. And then, miraculously, it didn't matter.

I had two blocks to go, and I knew that if it took me forever, I was going to finish my degree. I could see Mancuso's now—the red lettering in the oval window, the gold street number on the green awning—and I knew that in minutes, we'd be sitting in a warm booth and ordering something great. Maybe we'd sprinkle Romano on each other's soup. Maybe we'd laugh about the little meatballs. Maybe we'd look up at the portrait of those lucky, lucky people. Maybe I'd tell her the best one of them all, the time Big Dave beat Atlanta's Mad Mike Mercer, knocking him down one last time, but then helping him up, helping him up, and walking out of the alley off Atwood, never to fight again.

The Sammy Hall of Fame

I: Mrs. C. and the Pink Bowling Balls on West Third Street

A year after the sultry actress Adelina Oriopana drowned under an anchovy boat while completing *Fame and Fortune* in choppy Sicilian waters, her memoir, *All of Me and More*, was published, and the story of the Sammy C. Thing broke on Monday's *Oprah*, shot through the media, and then hit the port city of Oswego, New York, like lake-effect sleet.

By Tuesday, even the paperboy's little sister, Rosie Bosco, knew that Mrs. C.'s late husband, Sammy C., who fell over the back deck and broke his neck in the eggplant in 2005, had the fling with "the Queen of the B-Movies" in August of 1980 when she docked her boat at the Oswego Marina, where Sammy was working, rewiring the Blue Room at the Captain's Lounge.

Before the world had broken loose around her, Mrs. C. looked forward to these Tuesday afternoons when the Senior Ladies' League invaded her bowling alley with their pink balls, family snapshots, and foil-wrapped gifts of rigatoni, manicotti, or lasagna ("Anything but eggplant," they had been warned). But no—not any more. Since the story of her husband's affair was as undeniable as April snow, the bowling ladies took their shoes at the counter and quickly shied away to their lanes. Mrs. C. felt contagious.

And that afternoon, thanks to the *Palladium Times*, Mrs. C. was reduced to a front-page image: the jilted woman, her face flushed and frightened, the gray overcoat hugged closed.

"Thanks for meeting me on such short notice, Father," she spoke into the confessional mesh at Saint Joseph's church.

She heard Father John Zitelli ("Father Ziti" to his faithful) sigh twice. The first was heavy in disgust with the absurdity of it all. But the second, coming after a long pause, was lightened almost to a snicker by the unyielding humor that was his way of embracing all things.

He waited for her to continue.

"I feel . . ." her voice broke. "I feel naked and chased on the streets of my own city. What happened to *my* privacy? How about how *I* hurt inside, Father Ziti?"

He joked, "Well, Estella, now you're built for speed. That's all."

"That's all?" She failed to see the humor.

"Yeah," he assured her, "that's all. Come on, this will pass. Such so-called news always does. Paper: It's merely the thinnest paper to ashes. They chase you because they need you. It's more about what *they've* become than anything else. This is their city, Stella. You need to concentrate on the city of God."

She opened her purse, looked at her rosary beads, and closed the purse again.

He rubbed his chin and waited, satisfied that every injury was only a matter of brief human endurance born of perpetual forgiveness, all of it propelled to the infinite by the eternal force of humor.

Of course, that was wonderful in the *sanctum* of his confessional. But within minutes, Father Ziti was having another understanding entirely as he shot up the rectory steps to flee the reporter from the *Palladium Times*. The young man begged from the sacristy out through the back doors for a report on Mrs. C.'s confession.

Father Ziti huffed, "Confession is a sacred rite. Her privacy is unquestionably guaranteed." The multisyllabic words stole his breath, and his eyes bulged with regret. He collapsed inside the heavy door.

"So, there he was, collapsed inside the heavy door—you know, the one with Saint Francis and the animals carved into the top half."

Mrs. C. heard about the Father Ziti Thing that night from Gracie Spano, his housekeeper at the rectory.

Gracie brought over some gnocchi with pork steak cooked in the sauce. She dished it up, sat down, and looked terrified as she buttered two slices of fresh bread from Sebastiano's. "I don't know, Stella. Like I said, by the time I get out there, Father's got this terrible look on his face, like he wants to say something to the whole world, but he can't get the words out. Then he grabs the door knob and pulls himself up. He gives the reporter the finger, and then *bing!* He slams the door shut. But all the way down to his study, he's got his arms out to his sides, you know, just so, like one of those high-wire people in the circus."

Mrs. C. listened, her pasta going metallic. Slowly, she faced the fact that now there was absolutely no one left to talk to, not even her son, Sammy Jr.

Managing the alley since his dad's death, Junior was twenty-seven, engaged to a nice girl from town, and a graduate of Oswego State's Honors College. But Mrs. C. could hardly stand the sight of him since hearing that he laughed when the news broke, laughed and hooted with the damned hotshots in the Bowl-a-Rama lounge.

The hotshots: Mickey Zellone, Will Nuccio, and Charlie Meyers with the crazy ticker. They were all in the bar Monday when the Syracuse news came on, and the third story in was how Adelina Oriopana's daughter mentioned the Sammy C. Thing on *Oprah*.

80

They watched the clip of her saying, "Oprah, Momma said a world of love came and went in one glorious afternoon."

They saw the photo of Sammy C. Absurdly handsome, he smiled at them through time.

They watched Cindy Bonners from WSYR stand on the Utica Street Bridge only four blocks away and say, "Bob, a certain Samuel Castrioletta (aka, Sammy C.) is said to have had the torrid love affair with the infamous Hollywood actress in the summer of 1980. The Oswego electrician was apparently fixing the interior lighting on Ms. Oriopana's yacht when it was docked in the harbor under Fort Ontario. According to her memoir, she was supposed to meet famed actor Sir Roger Wilkins, but he was on a drinking jag at nearby Sodus Bay. We will have more on this fascinating story as it develops."

"Son of a bitch!" Nick boomed behind the bar.

"*Madonna mia!*" Mickey held on to his Yankee hat.

At his booth, Junior looked up from his paperwork, his one hand opening in a gesture of disbelief. He didn't know what to think. He searched the room for an explanation. For once everyone was spellbound. No great ideas. No suppositions. No prophetic outbursts. No sudsy theories from the hotshots now. No "Philosophy 101" as Nick called their heated discussions of sports, politics, or love.

Then, in one electric second, the lounge detonated into laughter. It was wild, wheezing, piss-your-pants-in-Sunday-school laughter. They reeled and rolled and filled the room with something that could've only come from West Third and Mohawk.

Mrs. C. heard all about the Hotshot Thing from her waitress, Viv Bellardino, who had been at the bar ordering drinks from Nick. She saw the pictures of Adelina Oriopana and Sammy C. flashing through the blue smoke on the screen, saw Charlie Meyers holding his chest like the next laugh would kill him but he still didn't care, saw Nick on his knees, sucking wind by the back-up booze. And she saw Junior slapping his table and high-fiving Will Nuccio.

"I *am* sorry, Mrs. C. But I figured you had to know. Junior ended up on the table swimming like a fish."

Viv brought over her homemade fettuccine with the white clam sauce. She dished it up, sat down, and shook her head in disgust as she grated the Romano.

Mrs. C. dropped her twirling spoon and couldn't shake the "flopping fish" image from her mind.

That Wednesday, Mrs. C. became a heroine for how she handled what everyone called the *Entertainment Tonight* Thing. Since *Fame and Fortune* was being released that coming weekend, the TV tabloid show invaded Oswego, and the small technical crew hid behind Mrs. C.'s rhododendrons. Buzzing over their heads was the neon sign of the seven-ten split being eternally picked up.

Mrs. C. rounded the corner, and they emerged—lights, sound boom, cameras, the works. The correspondent, Maggie Fillmore, came out of thin air to launch the same old questions. Mrs. C. stopped, her shoulders dropping, her long, exhausted sigh saying it all to America: *What the hell do you want from me?*

"Excuse me," she walked by Maggie Fillmore, "but I have a business to open for the day." Mrs. C. got the key in the door.

But when the crew pushed forward, breaking the archway enough for the glass doors to latch open, when they were actually inside *her* bowling alley, the fire lit through her arms and chest, and she turned to the children's ball rack and began rolling the pink and blue balls at them.

Over their feet, out the doors, down the sidewalk, and across West Third Street the balls flew. She sprained the sound man's ankle and scuffed the hell out of Maggie Fillmore's yellow shoes. On TV screens all across the country, Mrs. C. beamed with angry triumph and became a bowling champion once again.

Watching it on his TV, Father Ziti moaned and dropped his fork. That night, Gracie Spano made him the nice haddock with a side of green beans and garlic. He couldn't touch another bite.

But when it was over, the people from the neighborhood solemnly collected all of the balls in the midmorning heat. Not wanting to disturb her privacy, they placed them in the mulch under the bushes until Junior got there in the early afternoon. Cleaning and restacking the balls, he was surprised to discover that two of them were actually from the men's rack. They were pitch-black, and he had to grunt to heft them from the indented earth.

"Well, that's that," he had arranged the last one. "I'm about ready for a Sammy. What's good in the kitchen today, Mom?"

From behind the counter, she looked at him in vicious silence, her brown eyes darkening into a fierce squint. God damn it, she thought, if he wasn't his father all over again, all sweet-mouthed, honey-faced, and even more handsome in his boyish denials. How could he stand there with a crooked smile and ask her to make him a sandwich? But more than that, how could he have laughed? How?

She folded a polishing rag and bent out of sight storing it under the counter. Turning away from him, she sprayed shoe after shoe and wondered if she hated her own son.

II: Nick Behind the Bar: Counting the People

After years of soloing as the Relief Pourer at the Oswego Castings foundry, Nick Fontana had always worked alone. Observing people from that cool distance, he came to see himself as something of a philosopher. When he retired from the castings and started bartending at the alley, he felt placed in his element for good, convinced that he could discuss life forever while he was surrounded by the aromas of whiskey, cigarette smoke, and stale beer.

In truth, Nick was a considerate man and a deep thinker. That was, until he ventured beyond his usual one-liners. Then he got tongue-tied, his mind overloading with criss-crossed thoughts. Still, the witticism of, "Ah, I couldn't pick my nose!" was appreciated when Nick threw down his losing football tickets. And the sagacity of, "Ah, that guy couldn't hold his breath!" was praised when an "amateur" had two drinks and then stumbled out of the bar to the applause of the hotshots.

It was in this spirit of keen worldly perception that on Thursday, Nick placed a Jim Beam on the rocks in front of Junior.

"Thanks, Nick."

"Hey, kid, in this life, always remember, shit happens." Nick threw up his arms, "I ain't sayin' nothing else for the time being. But even the bible says that sometimes shit just happens." Backing away, he poured himself a rare midday Genesee draft. He placed the short glass off to one side, setting it down as carefully as a chess piece.

"Yeah, I guess so, Nick."

"Hey," he pointed toward the front of the alley, "okay, so she don't exactly want to talk to you right now. Hell, that's okay. That's her, what they call her *prerogative*. And your girl there, Peggy, she's a little pissed off at ya, too—" he stopped because Junior's face darkened at the mention of his girlfriend's name. "What I mean is, people forget, even their heroes, and nobody remembers what they had for lunch yesterday unless, you know, it's Lent or something."

Nick made his serious face as he sipped his beer, his moustache turning white with foam. He turned and threw up his arms, surrendering to the world on the other side of the mirrored wall. Nick thought it was a shame, just a shame that Peggy broke off the engagement because she, too, was disgusted that Junior had laughed with the hotshots.

"I don't know," Nick snarled, stepping up to the taps like a baseball player settling into the batter's box. "The fuckin' world's beyond me. I ain't got the words to explain it."

"Yeah, but you do a pretty good job trying. And don't let them shit ya, the hotshots in Philosophy 101 really look up to you."

They toasted. Nick topped off their drinks and began warming up to the idea that he should have a little heart-to-heart talk with Junior.

"Look," his eyes widened, and he pointed to the TV, indicating that his examples were coming from the real world. "If those sons of a bitches at the IRS can threaten to sue when they really end up owing *you* money; if some bastard can bounce off the side of your car, and then *you're* the one who goes to jail; if the bad shit can happen, then this sort of shit can happen, too. I mean, your dad has this Boat Thing with a famous lady one afternoon. It's dumb, stupid. But it's also, I don't know, *fantastic*. It's like a hundred-to-one shot winning at Vernon Downs. It's good; it's just bad timin' is all." Nick felt his logic slipping away.

Junior chewed some peanuts and knitted his brows.

Rolling up one sleeve, Nick pressed in: "He did a dumb-shit thing, kiddo. But that lightning that strikes our lives so fuckin' rarely hit him right between the eyes and blinded him. Just because it's dumb-assed, doesn't mean it ain't fantastic, and just because it's dumb-assed, doesn't mean it's all bad, either."

Nick's eyes were ablaze as he rolled up his other sleeve.

Junior looked over Nick's shoulders, where Mr. Douglas was having a discussion with Arnold the Pig on *Green Acres*, and the craziness of something somehow being *both* good and bad, *both* real and fantastic made him burst out laughing at the exact moment Nick had tilted his head and looked his most prophetic.

"Hey, kid, you're laughin' right in my face. What the fuck?"

"No, Nick. The pig. You know, Arnold. The TV."

But when Nick turned, the screen showed a housewife proudly getting stains out of her laundry.

"Sure. Sure." Nick grabbed his towel and circled it down the bar. Damn it, he cursed himself: He knew better than to drink so early in the day.

That night, Nick studied the *Palladium Times* and poured over both Syracuse newspapers. He kept a vigil on CNN and Headline News. He was counting the people, the ordinary people whose lives were hit by the sort of lightning he'd theorized about to Junior, the lightning of the world.

In an old composition notebook, he categorized: 1) Good Things; 2) Medium Things; and 3) Bad Things. He left several pages for examples of each kind of thing that could happen to the average person. This seemed remarkably philosophical until he realized that he didn't know what in the hell a Medium Thing was, so he ripped out those pages. Then he got underway, and in no time, the Bad Things were ahead, nineteen to six.

By the next day, the score stood at twenty-nine to ten. Surrounded by clippings, Nick shifted the pile, and there, frozen in the photographer's frame, Mrs. C. surged up Mohawk Street, her eyes gazing straight ahead, her purse clutched to her chest. Beneath all of the fear and anger, her face was still the beautiful Sicilian face of Estella Batista, the girl Nick watched grow up on West Seventh, the young woman who stunned Oswego by winning the Buffalo Open at the age of eighteen, and the graceful bride who danced with him at her wedding in 1972.

Nick looked at his notebook. It was almost ready for his little report and apology to Junior. This time, though, he promised himself, he wouldn't drink any beer. He turned a page, and the new picture of Mrs. C. flopped over his knuckles. He faced the question: Which was it, then, a Good Thing or a Bad Thing? He turned off the TV, so he could think. He thought of Adelina Oriopana handing him a cold Genny, her robe falling open to reveal dreams. But he saw Mrs. C.'s anguished face, and he changed the twenty-nine to thirty.

III: Junior, the Hot Bastard Kid, and the Sammy Hall of Fame

When the Bowl-a-Rama began dying a few years ago, Junior got two stellar ideas. The first was to start a college bowling league, complete with annual competitions and a state-wide invitational tournament. The second was to put in a kitchen and create a menu of only three giant sandwiches. These would be called "Sammies" after the monumental conglomerations of meat, cheese, and vegetables that Sammy C. used to construct.

"Eat one of these," he said on break one day, "and the world goes away."

The biggest train among the Bowl-a-Rama Sammies was the Hot Bastard, which held a pound of infernal sausage from Sebastiano's and a half-pound of volcanic Fresno peppers.

There were many Sammy stories, the most famous one being the time Will Nuccio's thirteen year-old son, Leo, took up his father on a bet and wolfed down a Hot Bastard in what turned into a rite of passage.

"Kid, if you can eat that, you get the keys to the '82 Caddy in the garage."

"You'll pay the piper to hell and back if that kid gets sick in my restaurant," Mrs. C. shook her head and left the lounge.

Sensing history in the making, Junior loaded the camera with film.

Sweat beaded on Leo's face as he stopped four bites into his assault on the sandwich, which stood as formidable as shoreline rock.

"He can stop. He can catch his breath, Willy," Junior focused his lens and announced the rules. "You never said anything about not stopping."

"Okay, okay," Will agreed. "But he can only stop three times. If he stops a fourth, no keys."

The hotshots and the others burst out laughing, and the bizarre competition was drawing a crowd.

"That's fair enough, huh, Leo?" Junior became the kid's lawyer.

Leo's eyes hardened as if they'd just left childhood behind. He dug in, stopped a second time, then took a drink.

"Keep the drink small, kiddo. Keep it small," Charlie Meyers warned.

Pushing onward, now well past halfway, Leo chewed and chewed and then took his third stop. Tears streamed down the sides of his face.

Mickey Zellone stepped in like a referee between two heavyweights. He raised his opened hands, keeping everyone back. In that silence, the kid let out a howling burp that resonated like the mating call of a walrus. Then, camera flashing, barroom jumping, Leo Nuccio finished the Hot Bastard. He stood panting, weeping, and wheezing, but triumphant.

The lounge was transformed, bowlers leaving their alleys to come shake hands with the "Hot Bastard Kid." Charlie Meyers cried when Will handed over the keys to the sky-blue Fleetwood.

Mrs. C. looked in, shook her head, and said, "You're all a bunch of simpletons."

Junior used three of the photos for a Sammy advertisement in the newspaper, and business boomed. However, after hearing about the Hot Bastard Thing, Will's wife, Theresa, left him for two weeks. Then she came home again, entering with two bags of groceries, and wordlessly prepared tortellini and meatballs. She set the pasta, bread, and wine before father and son. Neither one looked up once.

Mrs. C. said that the "Hot Bastard Kid" advertisement was juvenile, but she knew what the Sammies were doing to get the Bowl-a-Rama back on its feet, so she put up with it, and, what's more, in a matter of weeks, she found herself agreeing to something Junior and the hotshots had named the Sammy Hall of Fame. This was a group of pictures that would line the walls of the corridor between the lounge and the alleys. Of course, the first and highest picture in the shrine was the one of Sammy C. getting ready to come to terms with a sausage Sammy. There he was in his peach short sleeves, two cigars in his pocket, beaming as usual.

"Jesus," Mickey Zellone was almost in tears at the sight of his old friend lifting up the stuffed loaf of bread.

Junior put his arms around Mickey, and the others bowed for a moment of silence.

"Oh, for Christ's sake," Mrs. C. muttered as she walked by them and back out to the front counter.

But that Friday morning, after Mrs. C. had to sneak into the alley through the back door and pass by the image of her husband and the words "The Original Hot Bastard" one more time, down came Sammy C.'s lopsided smile; down came the Nuccio men looking like lottery winners; down came Carmen Basilio making a fist over a defeated salami Sammy. Down came state senators, police chiefs, and athletes sung and unsung, each and every one an ecstatic moron for one glorious moment. Down came the Sammy Hall of Fame.

On Saturday, Nick was glad that he had stopped by Sebastiano's and had the old gent anonymously send Peggy Rizzo the fruit basket. Nick finished cleaning the front windows and was walking back to the bar when he saw her and Junior holding hands in the archway. In his white shirt and in her yellow dress, they were something to see framed in the darkness.

Taking the back corridor, Nick had his head down, and so he never noticed the missing Sammy Hall of Fame. He bounced along in the hope that everything would be okay now, that Peggy would accept the simple apology he and Sebastiano scribbled out and tucked next to the bananas, apples, and oranges.

But when Nick got to the bar, Junior and Peggy were gone, and Mrs. C. sat tapping the closed notebook. Damn it, Nick thought, he knew better than to leave it there, and he dropped his head the minute she saw him.

"What's this, Nick? You forgetting how to make whiskey sours all of a sudden?"

He drew two short drafts and put a basket of pretzels onto the bar.

"Oh, God, Nicky. Don't tell me you're writing some sort of tell-all for the *National Enquirer*?"

"Naw, Estella. I'm not writing for the news. Not exactly. See, I was writing more *about* the news."

She sipped her beer and listened to him explain himself. But three sentences in, when he hit the part about discovering that he couldn't define a Medium Thing, he got tongue-tied, and she was convinced that it was harmless enough, no doubt a Philosophy 101 thing.

Opening the book, he took her through his research. First, came all of the world's Good Things: the triplets born to their parents in a minivan in North Carolina; the girl who floated down like an angel from a fifth-story balcony in Vermont; or the dentist who tackled an armed intruder in California. Then came all of the world's Bad Things: the wedding cruise that sank in Florida; the epileptic driver who veered into a crowded park in Delaware; or the biologist who was thrown from his car on a windy bridge only to be knocked over the railing moments after he had pulled himself to safety in Michigan.

"Christ all mighty," Mrs. C. said.

Nick turned the pages of his chaotic collage and did his best to recount the stories of the lives he had gathered.

Then Mrs. C. flipped the last page, and there was her photo from the *Syracuse Post-Standard*, wavy and buckled with too much glue. She looked up at him in silence.

"See, Stella, I was doing all of this to—you know—to explain to Junior why the whole thing was a Bad Thing, and not a Good Thing." His voice broke, and he saw her eyes fill.

Estella Marie Castrioletta listened to a man named Nick Fontana do his level best to say that they were all sorry for laughing, but that it happened so fast that they didn't know what else to do.

"It wasn't what we would really do—you know—if we didn't see it on TV like that, so fast and at one shot. Look, Stellie, the kid loves ya. I know that much. Maybe if you let him apologize—"

Touching his arm twice, she put up her hand to stop him.

"I'm throwin' the whole thing out right now." Nick tossed the book into the paper basket behind the bar.

She nodded and made her way through the archway and out to the front counter. She tried to busy herself with arranging and rearranging bowling gloves and cleaning towels and shoes, but everything was already perfectly placed, and every time the doors opened, she looked up only to look away more quickly.

IV: Sammy C. and Alley Number Six

Early Sunday morning, Mrs. C. was in her garage, standing over the covered boxes that once were the Sammy Hall of Fame. It was only seven o'clock, so she had plenty of time to make the three trips to the alley before Junior got there around nine.

When she crossed at Third Street, she heard the squealing brakes, and then the young reporter who had chased Father Ziti up the rectory steps hopped from his car and matched her stride for stride.

"Mrs. C.! Mrs. C.! You haven't given any statements whatsoever. All of this time, and people are still wondering. Couldn't I ask you just a few questions?"

"Go to hell," she said evenly, keeping her pace and holding the box closer.

"But the world wants to know what *you* have to say. After all, what *is* your response to this whole thing?"

They were almost to the Bowl-a-Rama. He was in the road, his car chiming endlessly in the distance.

"Your response has got to be more than just rolling bowling balls at the *ET* people. I mean, *Fame and Fortune* was released this weekend. I'm seeing it myself tonight in Syracuse."

"Have fun," she wouldn't look at him.

"Please," he had stopped walking.

She stopped and turned. The curb was elevated, so she was suddenly above him.

Beaming, he scrambled for his notepad and pen.

She took a picture of Boom Boom Mancini besting a meatball Sammy and let the blinking, stunned reporter have it over the head. The frame shattered to pieces, and the picture fell into the road.

Mrs. C. entered the bowling alley through the front door, locked it behind her, and set the box down on the counter. Her heart pounded wildly. She exhaled slowly, swearing that the Sammy Hall of Fame was going back up if it were the last thing that she did. On the stepladder, she balanced the poster of the Bowl-a-Rama. After hanging up the five other photos where she thought they went, she was face to face with her husband.

She turned on alley number six and put Sammy C.'s picture on the chair next to her. She bowled two frames before sitting back down.

In the humming quiet, she remembered Sunday afternoons with the three kids, their pockets stuffed with Nestle bars and Bazooka bubblegum. There was that one Sunday when Sammy kept rolling strike after strike. First, three straight, or a "turkey." Then, a "four-bagger," a "five-spot," and a "six pack." There was no term for seven in a row, only whispering over the lanes as his curving ball powered out the eighth, ninth, and tenth strikes. Even the kids stopped chewing and held their breath when his ball hit the headpin dead-on for the eleventh time.

Forty or fifty Sunday bowlers and a few more drinkers stood and gazed at a man who made the pins roar and shatter one final time. After that thunder, the ten pin stood stock still, defying any force in the world to budge it.

The alley broke into cheers at the near-perfect game, the 299.

"Ah, what ya gonna do?" Sammy C. laughed his way back to the bar.

And within minutes, the place was alive again with the soothing rhythms of balls rolling over the hardwood.

"Mrs. C.!" The reporter banged on the front doors. "You've *got* to talk to me now! You've *got* to give me your story." He waved the crumpled photo. He was bleeding.

She would get up and go deal with him. She promised herself that much. She would give him his damned interview. She'd tell him what was on her mind and in her heart. And it wouldn't be any kind of angry, bitter, eye-for-an-eye thing, either. Hell, she thought, the actual truth about a man and a woman might not even be news at all. Is it news that a man's face can consume a woman's life? Is it news that a woman simply wants her son to walk through a door?

Yes, she would go. She would stand up, unlock the door, apologize, offer a bandage, sit him down, pour him a beer, and then tell him a thing or two about love and goodness and bowling alleys on distant Sunday afternoons.

She would. But first, she wanted to look down the alley until she caught her breath completely, until the red second hand swept around the clock one more time. First, she wanted to stare down those long planks, all the way to the pins, and lose herself in the brilliant shafts of light that burst here and there across their polished surfaces.

THE ROOM OF ANGELS

There is a road, no simple highway
Between the dawn and the dark of night
And if you go, no one may follow
That path is for your steps alone
    —The Grateful Dead
    "Ripple"

    I: "Eyes of the World": When We Danced Our Dead Dance

*W*e turned those old couches and chairs into trampolines whenever Momma did her Dead Dance, especially once her ringed fingers and braceleted arms became the stories of the songs shooting through the faded red house at the end of Whitman Road. With only two hundred yards of woods between the collapsed back fence and the eastern shoreline of Lake Ontario, the "Plantation" as Momma called it could be lonely and desolate with its scrub pines, burning barrels, and crab grass. But not so when she cranked those Pioneer speakers, moved as if the sun had ignited the water just for us, and danced to the begonias blossoming at our feet. Jerry Garcia sang:

Wake up to find out that you are the eyes of the world

"Come on, babies, and dance with Momma," she said.

Then it didn't matter that the night waves echoing through the screened windows would haunt us for the rest of our lives. Then it didn't matter that the summer residents cast their sour faces at us as they powered down Lake Road in clouds of Lincoln and Cadillac dust. Then it didn't matter that our fathers were the poets, painters, and musicians Momma never married. No—jumping and singing and yet never knocking over a thing, we had our circle of laughter, and each time, I knew that this time, *this* time, it had to last beyond Jerry's mournful "Stella Blue," which Momma played last when the slow dances finally came, and we took turns holding her tight.

"That's it," she taught us to bop our shoulders and weave our hands slowly, up, up, up.

Each time we danced, I closed my eyes and wished that Grandpa, Momma's dad, never snarled at her, calling her a *whurre*, even though my gut burned laughing at the roller coaster ride he gave the word as he exploded with it like Yosemite Sam. Each time we danced, I wished that Nonna Pam, Momma's mom, stopped calling to tell Momma about the latest porcelain figurine she was adding to her Room of Angels, and then demanding that Momma quit her sinful ways and come and kneel in that sanctuary, so they could see God together. Jerry sang:

But the heart has its beaches, its homeland and thoughts of its own

Each time we danced, I wished that Momma would get a steady boyfriend and not be the pink-uniformed Tea Cup diner waitress who everybody in Oswego gossiped about, the beautiful auburn-haired woman who never recognized that beauty, the woman who supported a poet gas-pumper, then a painter trash-hauler, then a musician tire-changer, and then, when we were all a little bit older, a bagboy who wasn't a boy at all but a thirty-nine year-old man, even though I loved yet hated the way Grandpa and Nonna Pam tore the word apart the night they got wind of the situation, gave up their Oral Roberts's radio broadcast, and came bounding down Whitman Road loaded for bear.

"He's not a *boy*," Grandpa cried in the kitchen, his moustache a thick hook hovering above his upper lip. "He's a *man*. Got it, honey? He's a full-grown *man*! There isn't any such a thing as a bag*man*!"

"Well," Nonna Pam corrected him, "there are bagmen in the Mafia, but God all mighty in quicksilver, don't wish that on us. It's bad enough as it is without her sleeping with criminals, too."

My heart broke to the knives and fists and fire of their words, but it swelled to bubbling with the circus of absurd images that flew through the air.

They spat their anger room to room, winding their way to the front of the house.

"When are you ever going to knock it off with all of your *whirring*?" Grandpa went down the steps and was throwing his body into screaming spasms from the side yard. I could feel the walls shaking. I saw him balling up his fists and bending forward, his face nothing but moustache, the red golfing pants Nonna Pam bought him billowing in the lake wind.

He walked all the way down to the water and went into the black waves up to his knees, which wasn't that far since he was only five feet tall.

I ached for him yet bit my laughter to blood at the way he returned to stand on the front lawn hollering for Nonna Pam.

She told us kids, "Oh, don't let him bullshit you any. He was only two or three rocks off the shoreline."

When he came back to stand in the back yard, the lower half of his body was so black with wetness that from the waist down he was disappearing into the night. But Momma was already out there pulling him back into the world.

"Here," she said, leading him to the sewing room, where he could change. "I found these old pants of yours down in the laundry room just now."

Nonna Pam scrunched up her face because she had forbidden Grandpa to leave anything at our house since she intermittently exiled him from the Plantation and exiled Momma from their house for having babies out of wedlock. I mean, by Nonna Pam's rules, Grandpa wasn't even supposed to be there that night.

"Damn," his swim had taken ten years off of his face as he smiled the jeans up into the light. "I thought I'd lost these old things years ago, just years ago."

"Well, they're back now, so put 'em where you sit."

I loved Momma's one-liners. And I loved that we all knew she had produced those jeans out of the thin air.

But now, we danced, and Jerry's voice rose with his promise:

Wake now discover that you are the song that the morning brings

No—when we danced our Dead Dance, I wished that everything would stay like that forever if only everything would change there and then for all of us. There were my big brother, Bobby (named after both Robert Hunter and Bob Weir), my little sister Sweet Anne Marie (named after the lost lover in "Friend of the Devil"), me, Mickey (named after the drummer Mickey Hart), and our two pets, a giant prophet of a Newfoundland dog named Tennessee Jed, and a llama named Sugar Magnolia, who could take you into her compassionate eyes, and then, without blinking, dismiss you the second you got too comfortable there.

"Open your eyes. Open your eyes, Mickey. You're gonna fall down," Bobby yelled to me on the couch.

Momma turned it up, and Jerry finished the chorus:

But the heart has its seasons, its evenings and songs of its own

I never thought about what the words meant, but I knew from Momma, who never let us call her anything else, that if Jerry Garcia sang you something from his heart, then you hushed, listened to every string of that heart, and didn't ask any questions.

I opened my eyes so wide they hurt. I saw Sweet Anne Marie, her face straining because she lost her breath easily for reasons Momma never explained. I loved how Anne Marie said *wuulld* for world, singing it with an utter sincerity that should've bowed kings and queens. I saw Bobby, otherwise forever shooing me away, but now happy to hold me and even hug me in passing pulses. In one of my "moments" as Momma called them, I saw Bobby all grown up and loving men, at perfect peace in their arms. But I saw it cause him great pain, too, and I didn't want to see any more, so I hugged him tighter and tighter.

I made eye-contact with Momma, and she smiled. She was twenty-seven at the time, inheriting neither the fireplug shortness of her father nor the lamppost tallness of her mother. Like I knew she would, she held Anne Marie for the first steps of "Stella Blue." Momma wore a maroon tie-dyed wraparound skirt. Her hair, which could have fallen down her back, was up in a Grateful Dead rainbow clip. And her eyes— brown lights so intense that not even Sugar Magnolia could stare her down—they turned from me and then rose out the window as if they were seeing the lyrics themselves safely on their way across the deep blue lake.

II: "Box of Rain" or "It Hurts Me Too": Momma Is Shot

I tell you this story, sing you every last secret note of this song, because on a frigid January night in 1982, Momma was shot three times outside the Port City Tavern in downtown Oswego, shot three times in the stomach for writing a married man's name in the snow, or for helping him to write his own name in the snow, shot by his wife, who was the only person to gather there who didn't consider the perfect lettering a work of natural art, this despite the fact that all of the others said it was somehow glittering and golden and almost a statement about life itself. We couldn't help but hear all about it over that terrible year that followed.

The crowd at the Port City came out to gawk at the name in the snow.

WILLIAM.

All in capital letters. All engraved in the crystalline Oswego snow-bank. That's when the cheering went up. That's when someone lit a joint. That's when the bar brought out free beers (it was Molson Golden Night). And that's when the married man's wife marched home.

Everyone stayed there, the story goes, freezing but unable to look away from the name. Then they all saw the woman return. They all raised their green beers to welcome her. They all saw her draw the pistol —a .32. They all ducked when she missed the first two times, pumping one round into the outside wall, just above a joint-toking man who said, "Hey, what's up?" and then pumping another round that sailed straight past them, one person later said, heading right for Canada. And then they all saw her hit Momma three times. No one denied it, not even the woman, who fell to her knees in the same pristine snow-bank. One man later said that the night instantly grew blacker even though there wasn't a star in the sky already, but another woman said that that was only because the wife's final shot knocked out the overhead streetlight.

But no one had to tell me about the scene because I saw it all while Nonna Pam woke us up, stood us up, and wept the news. I saw Momma in the street, exactly like they would describe it later in the *Palladium Times*. And I saw one other thing, too, the thing that no one mentioned until it was well over: There was no blood, not a drop of it anywhere. Momma was shot in the snow, and the snow stayed white.

Because Momma loved the Grateful Dead more than any of them, it later became a sudden homage to her for the first two trial witnesses to recall what particular song was playing at the time of the shooting. To them, Dead Heads to the last, it was like Momma's funeral music, like Mozart's *Requiem* or Samuel Barber's *Adagio for Strings*.

In the middle of answering a question, the first witness suddenly offered: "And, wait. Now that I think about it, Your Honor, 'Box of Rain,' was playing. I heard it clear as day. My favorite part, too. The fourth verse:

> Walk into splintered sunlight
> Inch your way through dead dreams to another land."

As he sang, some Dead Heads swayed in their seats.

"Order!" The judge pounded his gavel. "Just answer the questions you're asked, please."

And then, during her questioning, the second witness burst out, "And Your Honor, sir, I know what Rusty just said, but that ain't the song. The song that played at the time was 'It Hurts Me Too.' It was the very first chorus:

But when things go wrong, wrong with you
It hurts me too."

The judge became outraged by the singing witnesses. But even he was moved by the third man, who broke down and swore to the statue of Justice that somehow both songs had played. "Oh, Your Honor, a tape-player miracle happened that night. That sweet and bitter night."

When Nonna Pam finished reading it to me from the paper, she stuffed the *Pal Times* under a couch cushion, so Grandpa wouldn't see it and cry.

"Now, this is between you and me, Mickey. That damned writer is plain sinful. He thinks this tragedy is all one big joke. That whole damned town does."

We peeled potatoes, and Nonna Pam led the Lord's Prayer for Momma. *Our daily bread, our daily bread, our daily bread . . .*

Still, I couldn't get the question of which song played out of my head, and I knew that if Momma had to pick, she'd choose "Box of Rain."

I saw her teaching us all about the Dead while we did our homework. I heard her say, "Elmore James's 'It Hurts Me Too' is one of the greatest blues tunes ever recorded." Then I could just hear her add, "But no one should have to die to a blues tune."

I remembered her showing Bobby how to do his math and then launching into, "'Box of Rain' was written by Phil Lesh for his dying father, and that song, like all great songs, wrote itself. Plus, it's *existentially undeniable* that this really *is* 'all a dream we dreamed one afternoon long ago.'"

When she talked like that, so smart, so sure, no one argued with her, not even Nonna Pam. Well—that was if it happened to be during a time when Nonna Pam was even talking to Momma.

Okay, Momma was the twelve year-old girl who cut school and broke into the Figure-Eight Roller Rink to spin in the morning half-light, and she was the fifteen year-old who ran away to the Syracuse War Memorial to see the Grateful Dead only to be dragged from the building by her howling father, who said, "You keep this up, Crystal Lee, and people will start thinking you're a *whurre*!" And Momma loved a poet who couldn't write poetry and a painter who couldn't paint and a musician who stopped hearing music and a bagboy who was really a man. But the poet rolled joints with one hand to celebrate rhyme, and the painter opened bottles of Old Vienna with his teeth and put pigments in the caps, and once upon a time, the musician brought a bar to tears with every note a dream, and the bagboy loved people with all of his heart, and they were all the very breath of life for Momma.

Oh, Momma told secrets to a gigantic Newfoundland dog, was drunk most Sundays, put Easter bonnets on a llama that acted cockier still because of them, and sure, Momma wrote a married man's name in the snow, a man who was named William, and when you're writing W-I-L-L-I-A-M with great caution and care and precision into the purest snow imaginable, well, you're holding onto something you shouldn't be holding onto for longer than you should. Sure, she wrote his name in the snow, but she never deserved to be shot, especially straight through her new *Terrapin Station* dancing-turtle tattoo. No, Momma didn't deserve to die because, you see, she was an angel.

III: "Friend of the Devil": The Woman in the P&C

"Here comes that whore," I read the lips of Mrs. Hollis in Customer Service as we stepped through the electric doors of the P&C, the wind of a coming lake-effect storm whistling in with us. This was the last time we went shopping with Momma.

The insult didn't bother me because I knew something special was going to happen to us that day. My stomach buzzed with it. Plus, I knew that Mrs. Hollis, a lady from our church, couldn't look Momma in the eye.

"Is Ronny Wilkins here today?" Momma asked about her bagboy.

"Why no, dear," Mrs. Hollis savored each syllable. "He doesn't work here any more. He moved." She returned to her paperwork.

Momma's face fell as if the snow outside whipped it one more time. But when she pushed our cart, she smiled as if someone were telling her a funny story that took some time to understand. She even laughed at the back of the store when the assistant manager said, "Hey, hi, Crystal Lee. Guess you heard about Ronny, huh? He took some sort of civil service job out in New Mexico."

Down the cereal aisle, Momma did a little dance and made the cart seem weightless even though it was nearly full.

When we rounded the canned-goods aisle, that's when it happened. A woman I will never forget passed us in such earthly gravity that the world stopped, and I could hardly move. Momma said nothing to Bobby or Anne Marie, but she looked at me in brown-eyed brilliance.

She asked wordlessly, *Do you see her?*

Yes, Momma, I do.

She is weight. We are lightness.

Yes, Momma. I understand.

The woman wore a thin green coat, its top button dangling like a broken yo-yo. Her eyes had stopped seeing, been turned to pale lake stones. I turned and gazed at the back of her coat: It glowed under the lights. Then I saw the woman's three children, one of them sick on a couch; I saw her house, a place down by the Oswego River; I saw a car outside, in the yard, up on cinder blocks.

Everything started again, and we moved forward. Momma never glanced back, but I knew she was going to do something.

When we went to check out, I didn't notice it right away, but the woman was three people behind us.

"My, isn't Mickey a natural-born bagger," I heard a cashier say to Mrs. Hollis at the Customer Service desk.

"Sure, natural-born, just not legitimate-born," came the whispered reply.

Momma put groceries onto the conveyer belt and talked with the customer right behind her, so I figured she couldn't hear. Plus, a horrible stringed version of "Breaking Up Is Hard to Do" was playing, and Momma would never do anything heroic to that shit.

No. I now know that I alone was meant to hear those women. I know it as surely as I know Momma kept looking at me with eyes for all time when Mrs. Hollis came over to our slot, stood by the cashier, and lifted her head suspiciously because it was time for Momma to pay the $88.92, and maybe there'd be trouble since Momma had bounced a few checks at that store.

Momma dug through her purse and made her face turn red.

"I'll handle this, hun," Mrs. Hollis relieved the cashier.

Momma peeled out a hundred-dollar bill and set it on the counter for Mrs. Hollis to pick up.

"Take the change from that, and then take this," Momma handed Mrs. Hollis a fifty-dollar bill, "and give it to the woman two parties behind me."

I saw Momma turn Mrs. Hollis's face into a prayer made of flesh.

"Momma, why'd you go and do that?" Anne Marie wanted to know as we were whisked away.

"Yeah, Momma," Bobby's voice echoed through the electric doors, "how do you know that lady?"

Back at the Impala, our "Garcia Mobile," Momma lit a Marlboro and was putting the groceries into the trunk. When the woman paid her bill, we wiped away our breath to see through the flurries that Mrs. Hollis was holding up her hand, motioning to the poor woman that no money was needed.

We clapped for Momma, Anne Marie calling her, "Brave, brave, brave."

"Hush now, and buckle up," Momma said. "It's startin' to come down like bad news on your birthday. Home's next."

As we pulled away, I saw the woman's hands fall to her side.

Momma popped *American Beauty* into the tape player that only worked for her, and "Friend of the Devil" rang out from the big speakers on the back window ledge. I knew I'd never see a more powerful calf than the one that broke through the long denim dress, the one with the sides slit a little bit more, even though Nonna Pam swore that if Momma didn't stop making her clothes into trash, then she could never come home again.

Cruising east on Route 104, Momma finished the song:

Set out running but I take my time
A friend of the devil is a friend of mine

If I get home before daylight
I just might get some sleep tonight

"Again, Momma, again," Anne Marie called, loving it because it was her song, and she always got to be Jerry's "heart's delight."

But Momma already had the tape on rewind while she changed lanes, hit the gas, and broke past the city line.

IV: "Truckin'": A Perfect Traveling Camel at the Figure-Eight

She may have been a high-school dropout who thought that Edgar Allan Poe was the most famous American poet ever to become president, and she may have been sinking in her ninth year of interstate truckers and onion farm muckers over at the Tea Cup diner, but Momma could roller-skate like great lake lightning. Anyone who knew her knew that.

She often took us to the Figure-Eight, and that's where we were for Sweet Anne Marie's seventh birthday party. After Loretta Lynn, Johnny Cash, and a Beatles medley, after the "Beer Barrel Polka," the Chicken Dance, and the Hokie Pokie, the kids started to drag themselves to the tables for ice cream and cake. Tommy, the DJ, who knew Momma from the diner, called over the PA for an adult-only skate, but no one took the floor.

"How about you, Crystal Lee?" Tommy boomed her name.

Bobby, Anne Marie, and a few of the kids in their party hats dug into their cake.

Momma's real name, though, detonated again over the loud speakers: It was so unusual to me, such a strange music.

"Ah, get outta here, Tommy." Momma waved the ice cream scooper.

Some of the others clapped and called her name, and even Nonna Pam joined in.

Momma licked some frosting off her fingers, shook her head, and sat down to eat.

"Hold on, folks," the voice said. "I think I've got just the song."

Momma's hands fell, and her face flushed when "Truckin'" filled the arena:

> Truckin' got my chips cashed in
> Keep truckin' like the doodah man
> Together, more or less in line
> Just keep truckin' on

Grandpa was next to me at the front counter. His mouth opened when Momma blew by our end of the rink, hair flying behind her.

The adults inched closer.

But a man there with his kids complained: "Now, look here, Tommy, that Grateful Dead thing is a druggie song. My kids ain't skatin' to that!"

Young and intimidated, Tommy moved toward the tape machine.

Grandpa turned from his deep squint and said, "If you touch that thing, Tommy Kapinski, so help me God, I'll break your arm."

The crowd let out a sigh as Momma flew along the boards in a Coffin, one leg extended and her head only inches from the hardwood. A few of the kids saw it and began jumping up and down.

Then Momma did a series of sit spins, and everything slowed in my mind as the place buzzed with arms and faces and voices.

Grandpa's eyes filled, and Nonna Pam stood, strained, and almost shouted.

Jerry sang, "What a long, strange trip it's been," as Momma twirled the length of the floor in a Traveling Camel, her arms extended as she appeared and disappeared in a blur.

"Oh, my goodness," a woman's hand went up to her mouth.

"Man," the complaining father breathed but then rushed his kids out the door, anyway.

"For Christ's sakes," Grandpa whispered.

And then, while I was still seeing it, it was over. Momma skated back, and Anne Marie thanked her for the present.

"What present?"

"That, Momma, that!"

But Momma was waving at some of the adults, inviting them over for cake and ice cream.

I could be wrong, but then again I'm dead certain that Grandpa never called Momma a *whurre* again after that Saturday afternoon.

V: "Terrapin Station": The Dead Jones Look
and the Dogfish Picture

Although Grandpa was the most conflicted Christian in human history, he wanted to sit up front those few times we made the colossal mistake of going as a family to the First Holy Church of Jesus's North Oswego. Once settled in the first row, Grandpa scanned the altar, pulpit to crucifix to choir, as if it were his sole purpose to uncover some deep and hideous fraud. On the other hand, Nonna Pam wanted to sit in the back, in fact, in the very last pew.

"If I get the last seat on the last Greyhound to heaven, well, that'll be just fine by me," she said.

And so, on those Sundays before she died, it fell to Momma to break the tie, and we sat up front. With Grandpa staring and Nonna Pam stewing, I remember thinking that Momma sat us up there, so Mrs. Hollis and her gossipers could see us plain as day.

"The only reason why you want to sit up front is to get first crack at that communion wine," Nonna Pam accused Momma.

But Momma simply smiled at such meanness. On that day, I could tell she was thinking ahead to our dinner and hoping that her own momma liked the pie we baked the night before with the Granny Smiths we carried home from the woods in our shirts. Still, I wanted, even prayed, for Momma to drain that goblet of communion wine. But she never did.

After Momma died, Grandpa and Nonna Pam took us to church every Sunday. I hated it like poison because I knew it was only going to trigger another week-long war between them. But I loved it, too, because it was the only time we got to take the Garcia Mobile anywhere, and the seats kept producing pieces of Momma. First, we found a ring, then a lighter, then a barrette, and finally a Dead tape I thought was long gone.

Now, Grandpa loved music, even some Dead songs although he'd never admit to humming "Ripple," "Casey Jones," or "Friend of the Devil," and he loved to sing in church. Trouble was he had a voice made of human gravel, and when he raised it above the concord of "Somebody's Knocking at Your Door," it sounded like a warning emanating from the bowels of frog prophecy itself. As he insisted that, indeed, somebody *was* knocking at your door, I was certain that the entire congregation would think twice the next time, maybe later that very day, when some poor soul came knocking at their doors.

"August John," Nonna Pam opened on him when we sat to dinner. "Must you sing?"

"Woman," he said, condemning himself the second he called her that, "I only go there *to* sing. The rest of it is pure balderdash. People taking your money and then trying to make you feel guilty about only being human."

"Oh, chicken tits!" Nonna Pam stood and gave him the Dead Jones Look, Jones being her maiden name. Nobody else in our family, not even Momma, could accomplish such a ferocious face. Maybe it was washed out of us by poets, painters, and musicians. Or maybe it was Momma herself.

We ate in the living room, and Grandpa, banished in his sinful doubt to the kitchen, was left to pick at roast beef and scalloped potatoes. Thus began his rehabilitation: a steady diet of *Morning Message*, a TV show that got him out of bed at sunrise; then *Faith of Our Fathers*, a radio show that aired every day at noon; and then the evening Oral Roberts's broadcasts, which came in loud and clear since they were produced across the lake in Toronto.

A few days later, he made it to the living room, where he sat at the player piano waving his fingers over the chaos of keys in Scott Joplin's "Maple Leaf Rag."

"Here," she placed sheet music before him. "If you can play that boozin' good-time junk, you can play this sacred song for Jesus."

I thought I'd wet my pants or choke to death not laughing at this. With her Dead Jones Look in full glower, she appeared beyond all rationality to believe that a man who couldn't read a note of music to save his life was somehow about to transcend that mere inconvenience and play like a possessed Liberace of the upstate woods to save his soul.

He lowered his nodding head and raised one hand in surrender.

She harrumphed into her Room of Angels.

The next day, we were outside with Grandpa. The man down the street was painting his house and piping "Terrapin Station" through his back windows. Grandpa called us over to the picnic table, where he had an old box of Momma's school stuff. There were pictures she drew with too much yellow, and there were writing assignments with words escaping in all directions. But the one thing Grandpa held up was a picture she had drawn of a dogfish. Under it, Momma had written: "To Daddy from Crystal Lee. This is our fish."

I heard Jerry's voice come from the trees:

> While the storyteller speaks, a door within the fire creaks,
> Suddenly flies open, and a girl is standing there

"One day," he began, "I told your Momma, 'If you get all of your homework done, we'll take this Saturday and go fishing.' Well, we ended up fighting this magnificent thing down under the Utica Street Bridge in Oswego. We both had to hold the pole, it was bending so much. You know, I swore for sure that it was going to snap right in two. But, boy, your Momma kept right on reelin' it in."

"What happened?" Bobby asked, leaning to see the picture.

"This big dogfish, or one just like it, Bobby. That's what happened. It surfaced, broke up out of the green depths, took one look at us, snapped the line like nothin', and then took off for good. I only saw it for a second, and I've never seen one like it since."

"What'd you do, Grandpa?" Anne Marie wanted to know.

"I said, 'Holy cow, Crystal Lee, what on earth was that?' And do you know, the next Monday, she skipped school and went to the public library to look through books until she saw what kind of fish it was. She was afraid to ask the librarian for help because she'd no doubt call the truant officers. Your Momma once told me that she was in there all morning, and no one saw her."

He passed around the picture. I'd never seen such an ugly fish in my life, but Momma had drawn it beautifully.

I could tell by the way that Grandpa looked that he wanted to cry about Momma. Bobby and Anne Marie fought over the picture, and Grandpa went back into the house.

In a minute they ran off to swing and play with the neighborhood kids. I leafed through the box, and suddenly there was a picture of Momma. It was one of those wallet-sized school photos. She was in third grade, just like me. Nonna Pam didn't like pictures of Momma in the house, so I wanted to steal it, but I didn't have any pockets in my shorts.

"Come on, Mickey, we want to go ride our bikes," Anne Marie yelled.

"I'll be there in a minute," I answered.

I moved toward the back door, thinking and thinking of where I could hide the photo. I cupped it in my hands like a captured lightning bug.

VI: "Cumberland Blues": The Angels Ride Piggyback

Grandpa shrunk, and Nonna Pam got taller, so I knew something big was going to happen soon. The less they spoke of Momma, the more I thought of her. She had taught me that looking at things was only the first step, that the secret to seeing was not in the thing itself but in the spaces between and around the thing, like all of the silences that surround a song. So I kept my eyes and ears open, certain that I'd see what I had to see.

Then it happened. We were up front on the left side of the church, where I liked to think we sat in memory of Momma. Bobby and Anne Marie fought over a root beer candy. Grandpa snatched it away and popped it into his mouth so hard that he started to choke. Panicking, he got up, raised his hands over his head, and lurched toward the altar. When he bent way over trying to dislodge the tiny barrel, he disappeared behind the front pew.

He shuffled in front of the pulpit and looked either like a man possessed with epiphany or a boxer reeling off of the ropes. Worry consuming her, Nonna Pam was right behind him, reaching out to touch him but then pulling back at the last second, I guess trying to let him free the thing by himself. She scooted forward but couldn't back up again in time as he bent over, pushing his hips backward. Within seconds, she was up on the small of his back, her arms hugging him for dear life.

My friend, there are moments in this life when we know that we are completely alive, and I now believed that Momma started sitting us up there, so this very thing would unfold inside of our souls. I never loved them all more than when Grandpa gave Nonna Pam that piggyback ride all the way across the stunned church. I saw Sweet Anne Marie dying young; I just didn't know that it would be alone gasping for air in the Syracuse War Memorial parking lot, where she left her inhaler inside a friend's lost car. I saw Bobby taking punch after punch from the bullies at school for being nothing more than a tenderhearted, loving boy; I just didn't know that years later he would have to fight for his life in a Rochester hospital after being stabbed outside of a gay bar.

But that moment when the congregation stood in complete fear and laughter, I was positive I would never see anything, truly *see* anything reveal its face to me again. Of course, I couldn't have been more mistaken.

"They're angels," I whispered to Bobby.

"They're fools," he shook his head.

The candy launched from Grandpa's throat, and everyone stared in silence, watching it land to shine on the transformed floor.

Even though they couldn't bear to look, the people were flooded with joy, washed free of worry, and released from sin. They saw God.

"Look," I said to Anne Marie, "it's God."

"You're silly," she said. "If Bobby hadn't fought with me, none of this would've happened. It's always his fault."

I loved her so fiercely that my heart burned.

But Nonna Pam was ashamed, and so we were herded through the huge front doors and stuffed into the Garcia Mobile.

Anne Marie found another Dead tape, shoved it into the player quick as anything, and "Cumberland Blues" broke like daylight from the speakers behind us, Jerry Garcia and Phil Lesh wailing away:

> I can't stay here much longer, Melinda
> The sun is getting high
> I can't help you with your troubles
> If you won't help with mine

"How do you get this infernal thing out?" Nonna Pam reached across Anne Marie's lap and poked at the machine.

"No, no, hun," Grandpa held up his hand. "This one's okay. Really. It's all about the workingman. I like this one. Let it play."

She made him keep it low, very low. Still, to me, the music couldn't have been louder if we had rolled down the windows to discover the Grateful Dead playing live along Middle Road.

Folding her arms, she gave one of her best harrumphs. They couldn't have looked more disgraced as we shot home. But I beamed in believing that we were the service itself. Didn't everyone see that from now on, there was no need to yearn and hope and wonder, no need for sorrow or longing or pain? Didn't we solve every mystery? Hadn't everything been revealed? I couldn't have been more proud of Grandpa and Nonna Pam for showing us heaven, even though I knew they wouldn't speak for weeks, and our lives would be hell.

At last, my vision came: I saw them for the angels that they were, and now my job was to tell them as much, and then convince them that Momma was an angel, too. I didn't know yet how that was going to happen, but I was certain that it would only come to pass if I searched every last part of the world for Momma's presence and never stopped seeing her in my head, even though sometimes I couldn't picture her at night when I closed my eyes.

We parked the car, and Nonna Pam bolted for the house with Bobby and Anne Marie moping behind her. Then the first thing happened that would let me convince Grandpa he was an angel: He snapped his fingers rhythmically in front of the tape player, and *Workingman's Dead* shot out into his hand.

"How about that?" He looked back at me and winked. But they weren't his eyes. They were Momma's, and she held me for a second of glory.

"That song ain't half bad. With the banjo and all, it's bluegrass, huh?" He turned back around. "You know, I can't have her burning it like she did all the rest." He slid it in his coat pocket.

Outside the car, I finished the song for him:

> I don't know now, I just don't know
> If I'm going back again

"Big words for a little man," he rubbed my head. "Wait until you get older, and you know what they really mean."

But I was already certain that I knew what the words meant. They meant the end of pain. They meant that one day, I would be able to forget the wise and patient look on Tennessee Jed's face when we dropped him off at the pound, a look that said he had known all along that Momma was an angel, known all along that I knew it, too, and he knew that great things would unfold to me, but first I had to skip school and break into the Figure-Eight, not to skate, but to sit and look out at the dark floor.

And I was certain that the Dead tape in Grandpa's pocket meant that he knew, too, that he would become a Dead Head the very next day, refuse to cut his hair, put on a tie-dyed shirt, resurrect one of Momma's albums from the burning barrel, and lead us in a Dead Dance in Nonna Pam's Room of Angels, where couches and chairs became trampolines, and not one porcelain figurine fell to the ground.

THE COOKING LESSONS

For the olive
Will sing with the wine:
The ripening light will inhabit us.
  —Pablo Neruda
  "In Praise of Oil"

I: Hands Olive-Dark and Gloved White with Her Intensity

*Y*esterday, Dar was almost nude, cooking behind my kitchen counter in her Big Dogs apron, a Saint Bernard staring patiently and sweet-eyed at me from under her raised, straining breasts, that line of cleavage suddenly there. Dar herself suddenly there!

I swear the whole place was transformed. Seemed like that old Brer Rabbit cookie jar was even twitching its nose at me. You have to be kidding me, I thought. Darlene Whitman is six feet from me, standing there virtually nude!

She wasn't wearing anything. Just herself under the apron I gave her when we first started having the cooking lessons, back before we stopped for eight months and then started up again. I had left the house for a while, but when I came back into the kitchen, it was just her standing at the counter, dipping the veal medallions into the big ceramic bowl as confidently as anything. As crazy as it sounds, I watched her hands, her dipping technique ("You dip too soft, the flour cakes up; you dip too hard, you tear the meat," I told her many times before). And God, her hands were beautiful, olive-dark and gloved white with her intensity.

She had asked me to go outside for a minute. She said, "Go on. Then I've got a little surprise for you."

So I paced in the backyard, cursing all of the lonely mowing I had in store for myself that weekend. I didn't know how much time to give her. I mean, I figured she was only going to cook something quickly, show off a little, create a veal scaloppine or a chicken Parmesan we hadn't planned. So I let about ten minutes go by.

Coming back in, I made some small talk about the cookbooks I'd left on the counter, I guess, or some new recipe my mom was trying down at the restaurant. See, I wasn't looking directly at Dar. That was my solid habit with her, and I couldn't seem to break it.

During those first lessons last year, *not* looking at her made sense because, after all, she was married to T. J. Kemp from the paint store in New Alex. Plus, she had gone to college for a while over at IUP, and I was a little intimidated because I'd dated two women who went to school over there, and they both dumped me.

I mean, sure, the first time Dar and I were alone, I couldn't help but look quickly and see the way that half-smile stayed on her face as if she'd just finished telling you a dirty joke and were waiting for you to laugh, too. I couldn't help but steal a glance and see the way her green eyes fell on you slowly but powerfully like they were making up their minds to look at you now and you alone, like they suddenly knew more about your life than you did. I admit it: I couldn't help but see all of that.

But I never looked at *her*. Even though we stood side-by-side at my kitchen counter, I gazed off into the food we worked with, and it became a safe place for me: It could take me to her, and yet it also had a life of its own, a power that pulled me back into the ingredients themselves. More than once, I lost myself in fresh basil or lived in a crushed clove of garlic, her voice mingling with the aroma.

She leaned forward to place the veal into the frying pan, and I'd never seen such bare shoulders. She positioned the medallions with her fork, just so, and when she moved back a ways from the stove, all of that light from the fall day came spilling in through the stained-glass windows in the transom above my back door, and she stood in the fragmented shafts of red and gold and blue and orange and green.

With the certainty of a master chef, though, she started sautéing the veal in drawn butter and talking away like nothing was different, new, or strange. She smiled, looking as domestic as a cooking show host in her cozy TV kitchen. But her nudity, that smile, and those eyes: They surrounded me. I don't know. I can't say it any other way.

"Can you come and check these veals—you know, to see if I'm doing it right?" She spoke at last, her one hand opening, the fingers perfectly still.

I fell in love with that hand. I let myself stare at it, drink it in.

II: Patsy Cline and the Barroom Pronouns

I first saw Dar the night her husband, T. J., played at my parents' restaurant two years ago. My mother set up the gig for him. See, the regular band had some equipment stolen at a Polish wedding that got out of hand in Export. My mother had heard T. J. singing a few times as he mixed paint and waited on customers. She thought he was cute. Anyway, by about nine o'clock that night, he was out there on our small stage, crooning his heart out in a glittering green cowboy shirt.

To show their support, Dar and her mother were all decked-out in suede cowgirl suits with pretty fringed hemlines, fancy boots, and everything. They sat at the end of the bar sipping some sort of radiant concoctions. It looked to me like they were sucking on fluorescent light bulbs.

Joanne came back, put in an order for sandwiches, and said, "You aren't going to believe these two women at the bar. They've got the whole place mesmerized."

And sure enough, when I peeked through the portals of the swinging doors, I couldn't believe it. After that, I found every excuse in the book to go out there.

"Enough already with the clean glasses and the back-up liquor, Jason," my father said, pointing to the racks of glasses and boxful of bottles crowding his space behind the bar. "Christ, you're worse than your mother." He never said so, but I knew he knew. Hell, everybody knew.

Most folks around town knew T. J. Kemp, too. He was a big goofy sort of guy, all long-legged, friendly, and on you like a puppy, except for when he was drunk. Then he'd go silent, start chain-smoking Camel straights, and turn into an oblivious, heartbroken singer, sad and alone in his world of paint store tragedies.

My father knew that T. J. drank.

"Why the hell did you go and call *him*, for Christ's sake?" He wrestled with each word, his face tortured as we joined the crew for dinner before the shift started.

"Oh, if he stays sober, he'll do just fine," my mom promised.

The others finished their plates and were gone quickly.

It was Friday, and my mother had made shrimp scampi. She heaped his plate.

"Yeah, well . . ." he regarded the sudden pile of seafood.

"And besides," she added, "he does that Johnny Cash song you like, the one about 'roundin' the bend,' and everything. You know his uncle down at the paint store says T. J. knows more than thirty songs by heart." She spoke with her head down, hoping the mound of scampi would do the trick.

"Well, let's just hope that he stays sober is all."

"Good shrimp, Mom," I winked at her. "Just right with the garlic and Soave."

I could see that he wasn't going to argue any further. That wasn't their way. Oh, they would come out swinging and have their little skirmishes. But they never pushed it beyond a certain level. Instead, they argued through body movements and facial gestures, like the way she tapped the spoon against the side of the serving bowl, or the way he twitched his lips before digging into his scampi. If it got worse, she cleaned the place top to bottom, vacuuming the carpet up off the floor in the banquet room, or he locked himself in the cellar and did an inventory so thorough that he became a scholar of canned tomatoes, imported pasta, and wine.

But damn if T. J. Kemp didn't have a pretty good voice. After a few songs, it became clear that he was playing his first gig safe by sticking mostly to Patsy Cline classics. And after a few more songs, it became painfully obvious that he had no intention of singing songs by anyone else. In fact, he sang Patsy Cline songs one right after the other, without so much as an introduction before one or a break in between it and the next. What started out as a nice little medley had turned into a nervous and rushed Patsy Cline barrage.

When one of the songs ended, I could hear the giggling from where I was in the kitchen. I figured that he was telling jokes or something. But when I got out front, I saw my father's head in his hands. And sure enough, Mom was making and serving free popcorn from the machine and running every which way to avoid contact with Dad, who took it to another level by polishing the glasses behind the bar.

See, as T. J. continued singing, whatever he had to drink before he arrived kicked in, and he forgot to change any of the pronouns in the lyrics. This got pretty messy when he belted out "She's Got You" and "Why Can't He Be You?" And the longer he sang without any kind of pause, the higher his voice got. Some people ended up thinking it was a comedy act.

"T. J., you forgot your wig, son!" A voice boomed from a back booth.

"Who wears the pants in your family, old boy?" Another voice chuckled not far behind.

T. J. closed his eyes and sang with an urgency I'd never seen. Patsy Cline's lyrics were his final testament before God. I still say he never heard a thing, hell-bent as he was on wailing his way to Nashville. I watched Dar shake her head and chew her drink straw to shreds while her mom looked around for the catcallers.

After his ninth Patsy Cline song, he drew a breath and announced, "Well, folks, let me take a little break."

"Yeah, a break to check his drawers!" Someone shouted, and the place broke up.

"Break my ass," my father set down a shiny glass. "Break? You're done, kiddo." He scowled as he stuffed some cash into a pay envelope.

Dad politely gave T. J. the money, but told him to go home. Mom shot from table to table, delivering more popcorn and passing out Slim Jims and bags of peanuts.

T. J. took his money and looked at Dar with that shimmer of accomplishment in his eyes. Dar's mother glanced around suspiciously, looking like a Secret Service agent working a presidential crowd. She got some regulars to carry T. J.'s drum machine out to his truck.

"Come on! Come on!" She barked, slipping some cash to one of them. They couldn't get him out of there fast enough.

People were up, pumping quarters into the juke box, dancing, and making jokes about the bright lights and big cities that lay ahead for T. J. But it hit me that the poor shit had no idea what was going on. What a debut. He turned at the door and held up the envelope, looking like he'd gotten the break of his career at Catalano's Misty Lounge.

He got another gig a week later, drank too much rum again, and the same thing happened. He lapsed into Patsy's voice, the voice he'd committed to memory. This time, though, he was out in Blairsville, at Mack's Roadhouse, where the crowd was a lot more tanked-up and dying for something like that to make their night.

Lori from the Misty was there, and she said that three songs into the Patsy Cline barrage, he jumped from the stage and smacked a drunk over the head with a microphone. Trouble was he hit a man who hadn't said anything, and T. J. ended up getting hurt pretty bad before it was all over. A while later, Lori told me that T. J. was drinking even more, and he was hitting Dar, too.

It wasn't long, and T. J. and his drum machine made the rounds to about every back-road bar in western Pennsylvania. He constantly improved, and folks said he'd get his break one of these days. He relaxed and got his pronouns straight, too.

"He thought it was such a big deal to play out of state in a bowling alley in West Virginia the first time he booked the Seven-Ten Lanes in Morgantown," Dar told me during one of our first get-togethers. She mocked him, but in a loving way: "'I'm outta state now, Dar. This could be my big break,' he says. Like he's going to gaze out and see a stogie-smoker from Memphis waving a contract while he polishes off an Iron City in a bowling alley on the outskirts of Morgantown."

She'd make fun of him, his outrageous vision of success, but she kept on cooking gourmet dishes he didn't eat, and she never got to the part where he stayed away for days or slapped her when she asked to see the money. And although it almost slipped out as she stirred onions and celery into fresh stock, she never got to the part where she stole her mother's car three times, drove to a few of those country bars in West Virginia, spied on him from outside foggy windows, drove back, and then ditched the thing four miles away and hitched home.

No, she didn't tell me about that, but Lori did. She said it was a hoot how Dar's mother couldn't imagine why her beat-up Olds would be stolen only to be left in the same spot in St. Bart's parking lot over in Crabtree. She couldn't bring herself to report it; rather, she said some prayers for her religious car thief.

I remember the slow night Lori stood in the kitchen laughing with the story. But after she left, I sat in the stockroom next to the kitchen because I loved Dar with such a trembling that it tore me up to picture her on those roads by herself. It was me and those ingredients again, as if bay leaves could tell a new story, as if the Marsala wines could keep secrets in their dark bottles.

I heard the empty humming kitchen, the fan still breathing over the grill. I looked out across the prep tables, over to the line with my entrée dishes piled shiny and high overhead. I was twenty-four. I was in love with someone I couldn't have. The place was suddenly rich with the lingering aromas of sauce, fish, and pizza, and the slight smells of the spices on the racks behind me. For the first time in my life, I felt in my blood what it meant to be alone.

III: Hog-Tied in Front of Mister Rogers

Dar had gone to IUP for a term after she and her mom moved to Pennsylvania. Dar had written an essay on poverty and won a partial scholarship in political science. My mom told us all about it after T. J. sang at the Misty that night. Dar's mom liked the place, stopped in for lunches, and they sat and talked.

Anyway, my mom's one of these people, all you've got to do is breathe a subject at her, and she's off to the library or bookstore, and that's all she's talking about for months.

I was draining an order of rigatoni one Sunday afternoon, and the steam rose to reveal my mother.

"Do you have any idea of the disproportionate ratio that exists between the classes and the cost-of-living index?"

I had a hangover, and didn't know what to say. I mean, that intellectual stuff freaked me out even when I was sober.

"Well?" She expected an answer with her order of pasta.

"Okay, Ma. That's good. Yeah, the cost-of-living index." I dished up a couple of extra meatballs. "Here. Tell them these are on the house. You want some extra sauce, too?"

She gave me a look like I was beyond hope, and she marched off with her rigs and spaghetti specials balanced high on a big tray. I could picture her lecturing the unsuspecting diners, folks pausing mid-stab and mid-twirl to stare up in disbelief at their persistent waitress and her learned opinions about middle-class spending habits.

I may have washed out with my mother, but at least I knew what I could discuss with Dar while we cooked.

"So, how's the college thing going?"

But she softly sang a tune from the radio and cranked up the heat on a lobster Newburg. "He's *got* to eat this one," she whispered, stirring the pan. "I mean, come on, it's lobster."

She didn't even know I stood next to her.

The lobster was cooked, and it would start to burn in seconds. I couldn't take it any more. "Here," I said, handing her the wine. "Flame it, already."

After the flames died away and she added her lemon and cream and the dish began its metamorphosis from absolute ugliness to beauty, I asked her again, and she turned and told me she was having it out with one professor and that her mom had narrowly avoided a shoving match that week with a department secretary.

"I was glad we sidestepped any trouble. You know, there's no fooling around with Mom when she gets pissed. She was a horse trainer in Idaho in the early 80's. Once, my brother Mitch got out of control, like when he was about nine or ten. He came at her with one of those little souvenir baseball bats. I'm telling you, Jason, she tackled him and hog-tied him with the vacuum cleaner chord right there on the living room floor in front of Mister Rogers, who I knew saw the whole thing because he blinked at me, and he never did that before. I thought, Wow! Better not mess with Mom!"

She laughed but then lost herself again in the pink creaminess of the dish, ready to be eaten instantly yet condemned to her freezer. Was she thinking about her brother, a kid lost to the music underground of L. A.? Was she thinking about her father, a man who came east for work all those years ago but never made it back?

T. J. stayed gone more than he stayed put, booking places further down in West Virginia or up in New York. Dar was running out of what money I let her pay me, but she kept coming over, kept chopping and mixing and stirring and staring into dish after dish. And I stayed up every Wednesday night arranging bowls and pans and knives, lining up ingredients, each in its perfect place on the dark counter. I couldn't wait for the sun to break over Keystone Ridge.

IV: Disgust Made Bittersweet by Degrees
of Forgiveness and Love

Dar's mother moved back out west to pick up with a guy she knew from before and to work promotions for a Wild West show based in Cheyenne, Wyoming. That left Dar alone to deal with T. J., and my mother had fewer reasons to break for lunch and dive into economics and politics. She returned to her Italian cookbooks, which she poured over like novels.

One Saturday last fall, I was in early helping to prep for a wedding reception. I went out to the bar to get some towels and heard my dad talking with Johnny Walters. I listened. Johnny had his head down, and there was a gravity in their voices.

"Yeah, but he *was* a pretty good kid and all," Johnny's head came up.

"Yeah, Johnny. A good kid. Just too loopy for his own good."

"He was with some woman twice his age. You hear that?"

"Yeah, she left with him after a fight with her husband."

The two of them drank and smoked slowly, deliberately, as if their silent nonchalance could somehow keep the chaotic world from breaking through the front door, as if they were holding fast for us all.

Nothing makes a busy kitchen sing like big news, and the crew chopped, simmered, and cooked away while flushing and rushing with the story. What the radio said. What Mike the Cop said. What fell through the cracks and was left to speculation. Wiping my hands, I watched the dance.

T. J. Kemp, our wayward crooner, was pronounced dead on arrival at Wheeling Hospital, in Woodsdale, West Virginia. He had gone home with a woman named Susan Flint, who not only fought with her husband at the Lucky Spot Saloon, but actually punched him in the nose on the way out the door. She was the last person to see T. J. alive. He dropped her at some hotel along Route 70. He crashed moments later, only miles outside of the city. And that's all the article in the Sunday *Dispatch* gave up the next day, no matter how hard I stared at the print.

I thought of Dar, picturing her sleeping at the time, how quiet her apartment was seconds before the phone rang. And I saw T. J. driving north, dreaming at the wheel as he rounded that merciless bend. Perhaps he really was headed home. Maybe he loved Dar, after all. The possibilities had to be torture for her—disgust made bittersweet by degrees of forgiveness and love.

I saw Joanne, Lori, and some of the other Misty waitresses moved to tears during the funeral mass. I sat in the back of Saint Bart's. It was a hot September day with the big doors open, the fans on, and the birds finally going quiet when the priest nodded his approval to play Patsy Cline's "Sweet Dreams" before the Recessional.

That was eight months ago. Then one day last week, my mother came back to tell me that there was someone out at the bar to see me. My heart stopped when I saw Dar. She wore a light blue and yellow summer dress, her skin glowing underneath. Mom took my apron. We sat at one of the side booths. Dad brought us over some fried calamari and two short drafts of Yuengling.

"I think I'd like to start the lessons again," she said. She bit into a ring. "This is good. Done to perfection."

"Hey," I said, "we bread it fresh ourselves."

She said she wanted to get some more experience, even take notes this time, and then apply for the culinary college at IUP.

"Mom's moving back, too," she said, sipping her beer. "Says she has no idea what made her move out there in the first place. I guess rodeo men are about the worst. It's hard to see how a bronco-buster can be a playboy with groupies and everything. But there you have it."

It was great to see her laugh and dip the rings in the red sauce. I loved the foamy moustache on her upper lip. I had counted the empty Thursdays. There had been thirty-two.

V: Veal Scaloppine, Linguine with White Clam Sauce, and a Salad

Like I said, I just didn't know what to do yesterday when Dar was standing there nearly nude in that Big Dogs apron. She started talking a mile a minute, and the way she turned up the burner, I knew the scaloppine was a goner. But it wasn't. In went the mushrooms. Then she flamed off the wine and added the *au jus*. And I mean, there she was, happy behind the shooting flames, all blue and tipped with orange, discussing renting a house, planting apple trees, going back to college, and all the time never missing an attentive stir of the finishing dish.

"Like I said, I have a surprise for you," she smiled.

"I see you do," I laughed.

But she ignored me, went to the back burner, and held up victory in a small sauce pan: "My own homemade white clam. Fresh clams, too, from Wholey's in Pittsburgh."

She put the pan back, and I never saw a curving back so dark and beautiful and sliced with light.

Then she spoke slowly, "Hey, you want to come back here and drop this linguine?" There was the slightest quiver in her voice.

I felt the heat of her body as I stood next to her bending the pasta into the boiling water.

"You forgot a little oil, and some salt for taste," she pointed to the cruet on the counter.

"That enough?" The oil beaded up, and the linguine was curling under the water. I poked it with a fork.

She held my hand, "Honey, that's gotta cook a while, even for *al dente*."

She took the fork, set it down, and kissed me. I couldn't believe the softness of her mouth. I opened my eyes and saw every heartbeat of her face.

"There's a salad in the fridge. Why don't you dress it, and we'll eat in a few minutes. Okay?" She smiled as she said, "dress it."

"Sure," I could breathe again.

"Good," she glanced at the linguine and then nodded at me like an approving instructor.

In the refrigerator was the old wooden bowl filled with lettuces, tomatoes, red peppers, garbanzos, and Kalamata olives. It almost seemed a shame to pour the olive oil and balsamic vinegar over it. I had no idea what would happen. I couldn't see the future, and I didn't care. I simply saw olives. I saw her pouring Chianti. I saw the great salad, all the green and red and orange and yellow. All of it light. I was dumping and shaking and mixing with my old friends salt and pepper and garlic and basil, all of them blending like voices in a song. I looked at the ingredients, and I looked at her, beautiful, consumed in her cooking. I busied myself, too, every salad I'd ever tossed flashing in my mind while this one, *this* one, came to life on the big silver spoons in my hands.

She Left with the Bear
(Homage to Isaac Beshevis Singer)

> But when you're married the husband's the master,
> and if that's all right with her it's agreeable to me too.
> —Isaac Beshevis Singer
> "Gimpel the Fool"

I: Sitting at the Bottom of River Road, Venison Lick, PA

I was parked in my car, there at the end of something called River Road, trying to decide what to do next. I was a mild-mannered man, and therefore no match for what was up there. Of course, the car was at the bottom of a hill. It had to be. After all, I was in southwestern Pennsylvania. If you weren't on the top of a hill, you were either on a hillside or else at the bottom of a hill. If you weren't in some sort of specific relationship with a hill, all you had to do was hold on, and in a few more minutes, you would be. It was that simple. Hills, hills, hills, hills, hills. Oh, and there's not a river anywhere in sight of River Road. Liars.

Oh yeah, I knew that they were up there—my wife, Minnie, and the Bear—up there in their little pealing pink castle on top of River Road. And, of course, they were surrounded by trees. What else? This was southwestern Pennsylvania. The trees came with the hills. Trees and hills, hills and hills, hills and trees. If you weren't in the trees, you were momentarily outside of the trees, and, if you were by chance to worry about losing sight of the trees, all you had to do was give it a few

134

minutes, blink, and *poof!* You were back in the damned trees again. It was just that simple.

While another love song faded in and out from Pittsburgh, I tried to count the trees inside the passenger-side window pane. I searched the car for a computer manual to read. Anything. Anything but hills and trees and fading songs and Minnie and the Bear.

II: Big Jerome, Mitch the Chevy Guy, and Several Sailors Ago

We were from Eastport, New York, where I loved my computer job, and where there were no bears, at least none that I ever saw. And our splendid landscape was (now, how can I say this?) beautifully flat, even magnificently manageable with the sunset igniting Lake Ontario in the evenings, spilling all of that orange-platinum light to our feet as Minnie and I sat with Molsons and guitars along the shoreline. I mean, we counted the sailboats, and Minnie sang them love songs, for crying out loud. Sonny and Cher. The Beatles. Red Hot Chili Peppers. We knew all of the words, too. We were ecstatic doo-wop hummers and strummers of strings.

Sunsets, beers, guitars, and "I Got You, Babe"—yeah, sure, but no bears, not a single hairy one.

"Let's go for a walk," she said, and the woods became a flitting of sparrows, robins, and bluebirds.

In the afternoons, I read my computer manuals and handbooks, and I cross-referenced to my heart's delight. In her black thong bikini, Minnie stretched out all golden and glistening with oil. She gazed so adoringly at the nearing sailboats, and the fishermen and sailors stood up in their crafts and noted the rock formations through their binoculars and telescopes. She helped them in their studies by excitedly pointing out the cliffs on either side of the port just ahead.

And as day began its close, the stilled streams that fed the lake came alive with dancing catfish and trout. I arrived at the deepest understandings of hard drive designs, and Minnie took herself for a quiet two- or three-hour spin into town and back.

"Is that all you're wearing—that fish-net wraparound? You'll catch cold."

"Oh, it's still way too hot to catch cold," she said. "I just want to swing by the docks and see the pretty boats."

Yes, I was lord of my castle, and Minnie was my lady. We were both at one with nature. Oh, what paradise, what blessed bear-free days.

But then we moved here to Venison Lick, Pennsylvania, where my computer job was better, sure, but where the lakes were all (now, how can I say this?) man-made, and every damned place we went was uphill. Okay, okay. I know it. I got geographically bitter. I promised myself that wasn't going happen. I'm sorry.

Look, let me take a break to catch my breath before I go on. I know John Cheever did that in "The Fourth Alarm," where his narrator paused to get a drink of gin. I never understood it back in my college literature class, but I get it now. Excuse me while I stretch over here to get a Stoney's from the case in the back seat.

Damn. I forgot. These aren't twist-off. I'll have to open it with my teeth. Just because I'm short without being frail and have soft doe-like eyes, that doesn't mean that I can't open a real bottle of beer with my teeth. I was taught the trick years ago by Big Jerome, an American-Indian friend of Minnie's from the Onondaga Nation up near Syracuse. I used to love how he showed up at our parties suddenly with a case of Genesee under his arms like a stack of books, except that Big Jerome was a lot like Minnie in that he didn't read books. I often wondered what they did, then, with their spare time, and I pitied their lack of true understanding, their limited knowledge of the nature of things. Big Jerome—or B. J. as Minnie called him—was a great guy. I can't tell you how often he knew there was trouble in the house even before I did. More than once, I left work early and rushed home, so I could work on my hard drive research—and, *blam!* B. J. was already there, all sweaty and huffing behind the furnace, or breathless under the downstairs bathroom sink with a screwdriver, a wrench, or a pair of pliers flailing away.

"Man," I told him one time, "and to think that the landlord just had those pipes fixed."

"Ahhh," he snarled out his assurance, "those landlords don't know what they're doing."

"Huh, and I thought he was a professional plumber."

"Ahhh," he barked out his assurance again, "those professional plumbers don't know what they're doing."

As I surveyed the gleaming pipes, I was amazed: He had done such a fantastic reassembly job that it looked like he hadn't touched a thing.

"Hey," I asked him, "where are your pants and shirt?"

"Ahhh," he growled out his assurance one more time, "I work best in my drawers. Can't be ripping my clothes on important jobs, ya know? I mean, you're a computer expert. You know the high cost of clothing."

I stood there beaming like a fool, thinking how lucky we were to have a friend like Big Jerome, time after time, so Johnny-on-the-spot for us, and I wasn't even sure that Minnie knew he was in the house because she was up in the shower singing away. Yeah, you would have loved old B. J. Whenever he was in my house, his face could only smile.

He was bigger than life, a real bear of a man. Damn—there it is again. Everything leads back to bears. For Christ's sake. It's like I'm in the Bear Ring of Dante's Bear Hell.

Excuse me.

Ah—warm but good.

There. I feel a little bit better. You know, I don't mind being alone. Really. I mean, we come to our deepest insights when we're by ourselves, at our furthest distances from all that is seen or imagined. We trust in all we know and believe in, and we reach that moment of perfect seeing or imagining, perfect being, all of it in a flood of intuition. I keep trying to get there, but every time I come close, I only see a parade of bears—you know, Yogi-style with picnic baskets and stringed balloons, the works. But I could stay parked here for days. I don't mind. This Caprice Classic feels like a house, and I'll bet, if you had to, you could sleep three in that spacious, well-worn back seat.

"Just like a Cadillac without the gingerbread," the salesman said as he walked us toward "Valentino" on the day we bought it.

Minnie had made the appointment in Oswego for us to see the car, forgetting, I guess, that I had to make a presentation at work that afternoon. The hulking salesman was so happy to see us coming that he never even introduced himself.

"It's like a damned couch back there, huh?" He beamed at Minnie from the front seat as we pulled out for the test drive.

"Man, what an engine," I said. "Purrs like a kitten."

"Yeah, a kitten," he turned all the way around to face Minnie.

In the rearview mirror, I could see her fixing her hair and lifting her skirt to get more comfortable. She put on some more lipstick and perfume and seemed to be double-checking for something in her purse. Boy, if I told her once, I told her a thousand times that she didn't need to get all dolled-up just for me. But she seemed to want to look her best whenever we met new people. But me? I loved her the way she was. I mean, all of that wax and paint—it just shines up the surface of a woman. The real essence is what's on the inside.

"You're my Aphrodite," I told her once when she sun-bathed.

"You're Afro-what?" Minnie said as she got the camcorder and rushed off to film the two Athenian ships that were docked in the port. One of them carried the Greek National Soccer team, and the paper said their goalie stood just under seven feet tall. That Minnie—she just loved to live in the moment.

Anyway, I drove the Caprice for a while, and then we switched places, Minnie deciding to give it a whirl. When she gunned it, my head flung backwards.

"You'd probably have more control if you went ahead and took off those spiked heels," the salesman suggested.

At the next red light, Minnie passed her shoes to him.

"Wow!" Minnie said when the light changed, and we blasted through the intersection. "I really feel like I could go places in this thing. Let's name it 'Valentino.'"

"Sure," said the salesman.

That was so cute—Valentino.

"Hey," she asked him, "how much time do you have, honey? I'd like to see what this thing will do out on the Thruway. You know, see if it breaks a sweat."

"Hell, yeah," his voice was muffled because he was kissing her shoes for good luck or something, "breaks a sweat."

"But Minnie," I protested. "You know I've got to go in to work later on. I don't have time for the ninety minutes it'll take us to get out to the Thruway and back again. I need to give that presentation on the interior relationships of circuitry. These idiots who represent us can't see the forests from the trees. You know what I mean?"

"Yeah," the salesman said, "forests and trees. Sure." He was pressing Minnie's shoes into his lap, I guess to keep them from losing their form.

"Well, okay then. It's settled. I'll drop you off at work, and Mitch and I will give it a spin on the Thruway. You don't mind, do you, Mitch?"

"Hell, no. Anything to make the customer *completely* satisfied. That's my motto. I'll even pay the toll this time around."

"And then the next round's on me," Minnie joked.

I'll never forget how beautiful she looked in her black miniskirt and silk stockings. To relax a little bit, she even let down her hair, and it fell in blonde rivers onto her bare shoulders. Her blue eyes burned so adoringly that I knew she was going to love the car and everything it had to offer. And sure enough, we not only got the car, but we got it for a thousand dollars less than the asking price.

So, now do you see what I mean? I felt like a king. I mean, we were happy, really happy. And who can dare question such a life as that? My interior hard drive designs were all big hits at the company, too. My supervisor kept telling me that I was on the brink of a great discovery. He even said that no one had a deeper understanding of the theoretical constructs of circuitry. I mean, no matter what we did, things just kept coming our way.

But now this. Now, the Bear.

III: Meeting the Bear

The first time we saw the Bear, we were, oddly enough, standing on a hillside that ran along a man-made lake. And, okay, it *was* beautiful

140

back there in those dense emerald woods of Westmoreland County. The Bear was at the bottom of the hill. He had just come through a clearing.

Joe, the owner of the place, said, "See that guy down there, the huge one? That's the Bear. I was hoping that he'd make it. You know, he survived a moose attack up on the Yukon River. And he chewed a man's thumb clear off in a bar fight up there, too. Weird thing was they never did find that guy's thumb. The Bear don't say much, but he's good people. He moves trees and boulders in the remote back woods for the lumber companies around here. You know, he clears out new territory."

"You're kidding me," Minnie gazed at the Bear as if he were a distant Grecian ship. "He really chewed off a man's thumb?" She looked so sweet in her slit blue-jean skirt and yellow see-through halter top.

"Sure did," Joe said, flipping the burgers on the grill.

Regarding us from a distance, the Bear rose taller and sniffed the air. His shirt fell open as he ambled nearer. His loping pace picked up as the food was brought out and set on the tables.

He was a popular guy, and everyone flocked to him. He laughed deeply and greeted them by opening his hairy arms for big hugs. One hand engulfed a can of Foster's beer, and his thick brown locks flew free as he shook his massive head in delight. One of the women fed him a pickled egg. It disappeared like a coin into a slot. He gave her a burly purr of happiness. Minnie let out a low, bone-deep moan. When I turned, she quickly hummed the song that was playing.

Later that night, I rounded a corner, and Minnie was smoking the Bear's eight-inch cigar and punching him in the stomach. How odd. She never punched people in the stomach!

They made their way to the back steps, and she climbed them until she was as tall as the Bear, who stood in the yard. "Come on in here, you big old bear," she growled the invitation.

"Naw, ma'am," he rasped. "I ain't much in a house. Might take to disturbing things."

Thunder rumbled in the back of her throat. I lost it once someone turned up the music, and the whole place sang Joe Cocker's "You Are So Beautiful To Me." The Bear couldn't master the words, but she got him to hum along. It made me crazy.

IV: Bear Stories in the *Post-Gazette* and Moose for Dinner

About a week later, I woke up with my heart pounding out of my chest. What was that noise? Next to me in bed, my beautiful wife, Minnie, was snarling.

"What the hell's going on?" I asked her.

"Just clearin' out the old pipes, I am!" Minnie barked. Then she slapped my ass, and that left a welt that stayed for two weeks.

How odd—Minnie never barked!

That morning, she was captivated by a bear story in the *Post-Gazette*. You know, it was back in the fishing and hunting section of the Sports pages. She breathed heavily, giving a self-satisfied rattle as she took the paper into the bathroom and shut the door with a thud. That was so strange. I mean, Minnie loved athletics. I always knew that. But she never actually read the Sports pages.

At dinner, she stood over me smelling ripe as she slapped down a four-inch steak of some kind onto my plate. The meat flopped over the edges, Fred-Flintstone style.

"What's this?" I asked.

"That's yur grub, laddy!" She sounded as if she'd eaten a rusty bicycle chain.

"This must weigh five pounds," I protested.

"Aye, that it does, sonny boy. That it does! Just a piece of moose I rustled up this AM! Ain't no sissy moose too big fur my pan, by gum!" She bellowed like a buccaneer.

"Honey, what the heck's happening? You never bellow."

"You best just commence to eatin', and don't ya be a-jawin' ta me with yur sas!"

"Moose? Where'd we get moose?"

Her face darkened. She was right over me now, stark naked and with increased body hair. She tapped the big knife against the huge pan. So I ate it as fast as I could.

For the next few days, I chiseled away at my plate of moose, and I read every last word of the *Post-Gazette* Sports section. I noticed that bear stories inched their ways forward from the back pages. Sure, it's normal to see such hunting and fishing stories in the final Sports pages of any newspaper. But this was clearly different: Each day brought bigger and bigger bear stories, larger and larger bear photographs. It hit me: The whole world was changing.

I couldn't think at work. A few times, I even lost my way coming home at night. Minnie disappeared for hours at a time, saying that she was going to meet friends at the Ram's Head Saloon. I knew better, though. I drove by, and her car wasn't there. I think all of that moose meat was making me dizzy. I tried to focus on the bear stories. I reread them at night under my sheets with a flashlight, but they were hard to follow. It seemed there was an inexplicable explosion in the bear population, and regional hunters kept shooting at but missing the damned things, and a few had even knocked on people's front doors before walking off with food and furniture and televisions. The next day, the front page held the biggest bear story and photograph of them all. It was that guy from the deep woods near Joe's house—I swear it. It was the Bear.

V: Stopping Completely, the World Began
Again with a Side of Pasta

Then in one deep breath, the world stopped completely inside the Caprice. The radio went dead. Not even a static whisper of a ballad. There were no tunnels in the imagination, no songs to anticipate fading and returning again. There was nothing to count or read or guess. All thought wound itself down to the Bear sitting on a hill inside my brain. I couldn't hear heartbeat or wristwatch. It was in that minute that I looked up and saw them both clear as day, and I said my small good-bye to Minnie.

Yes, at last, I saw it all. Big Jerome winking to Minnie as he chewed the top off a bottle of Genesee. Mitch, the Chevy guy, nodding to Minnie as he fondled her shoes. But most of all, I saw myself: the eternal fool. And, man, on top of that, did I have to piss. I had downed three beers in that sweatbox Caprice, and as geographically bitter as I had become, I took some small yet final pleasure in hosing down the landscape.

In the weeks that followed, our separation became legal, and divorce was only a matter of time. Still, it takes a while for the brain to catch up to the heart, so falling out of love is like that slow descent in dreams—only when you *do* eventually hit the ground, you realize that you're still alive, and it's as if some angelic bird had pried your eyes degrees further than you ever thought they could open. Slowly, you stand up to see that the world has started again, and it has done so only for you. And then, although you never thought that the pain would lift, one night at the Ram's Head Saloon, the draft tastes sweeter than ever, and someone slaps your back during a joke, and in one hiccup of fate, every last heartache flies up into the smoky rock 'n' roll air.

Because Venison Lick was such a small town, and because I had been babbling heartbreak at the Ram's Head, folks shied away from me as if I were the hobbled one in the herd. Everyone knew that Minnie had left with the Bear. Plus, who can blame them? Nobody likes a guy who can't chew off his leg, lick his wounds, and get back on with it.

Then, after the birds pried open my eyelids, and after the bear stories took their rightful places again next to the turkey and fish stories in the back of the Sports pages, lo and behold! One night, my friend Goat invited me to a party, and in slinked a woman named Fawn.

In my new angel-bird peace, I could hear great wisdom in the simplest things that people said. I could hear it because I was focused and still and rooted to the spot upon which I stood on Goat's linoleum floor. Someone said, "These extra-thick potato chips are the best." But I heard, "The world will be wonderful once everyone turns and looks into the eyes of the nearest human."

I could see the world before me, and I could imagine the world around me.

And that's all there is, and that's why I fell in love with Fawn when she spoke these words: "There are two kinds of women in this world: There's the kind that will stay inside all day Saturday and make homemade pasta, and then there's the kind that won't. That's it. And honey, I will."

Fawn, the pasta girl. I loved her head to toe.

That spring, flowers blossomed, and streams ran strong. Fawn graced my yard by walking across it with the last box of her pasta equipment as she moved in. She fed me homemade linguine, gnocchi, ziti, and rigatoni. I gained back all of the weight I'd lost on the moose diet. I never brought home work again, and yet I invented the T-57 circuitry used in hard drives around the world. It's been called one of the greatest computer inventions of the decade, the ultimate integration, and I saw it all in a flash of Fawn's eyes as I twirled angel hair pasta. It came to me in a strand that moved in clam sauce.

Oh, for a time, I still hated the landscape of southwestern Pennsylvania, its hilly roads and man-made lakes, and I still slid off the snowy roads and got stuck coming up my own driveway. But, you know what? There are a lot of natural rivers to love, especially the confluences, and a fella can overlook a man-made lake now and then. And so what if I had to abandon my car part way up the damned driveway every night and walk the rest of the way and sprain my ankle once in a while? On my crutches, I learned to let it go, and, in short, I lost my geographical bitterness, and the place became beautiful.

In the end, the divorce became final. We signed our names to lots of papers, and the Bear even sat out in the lawyer's waiting room and doodled on a pad Minnie had bought him, pawing out his rough-hewn poems. He had enrolled in writing courses at the Venison Lick branch campus of Penn State. I had to admit it: I was quite impressed with what he'd become. Minnie apparently met him halfway: She let her eyebrows sprout like Brillo pads, and he slept indoors—well, at least on the coldest nights. Still, as I turned at the door, I saw Minnie giving a woolly caterpillar of a wink to her lawyer, and I could only imagine where that would lead.

A few months later, I ran into Minnie downtown at the bakeshop. She said that she wanted to come home, that the Bear had been writing incomprehensibly mournful love poems for months, and that he had run off with his English professor, a woman called Ms. Bookbinder.

"My life is set now, Minnie," I told her. "I'm getting married on a hill by a lake in the deep woods, and Fawn will be opening up the swankiest Italian restaurant Venison Lick ever saw."

"Oh, I see," she purred sadly. She was trying. She'd even shaved her eyebrows. "You sure?" Minnie winked.

"Yeah, I'm sure."

I offered her a little bit of money and said that she could have the Caprice, too.

She said thanks but no thanks. But I knew better. I left the Caprice at the bottom of the hill below her new house, and I stuffed a couple thousand dollars in the glove box.

I made sure to drive by it on my way to work each day. Soon it sat perched at the top of the hill.

Then I was on my way home from work one night, and I stopped at the intersection of Routes 22 and 819. Minnie and some man were opposite me, stopped in the Caprice. She was with this one guy called the Fox. He'd been in jail a few times as I recall. His red hair was slicked back in thick waves, and his eyes glowed as he played a mean fake-piano over my old dashboard. Minnie looked happy as hell. Funny thing was her bouncing hair had all of these reddish highlights now, too. They sang some sort of love song. I couldn't make out the words, but their voices carried them in unison. Strange, I thought, but that radio hadn't worked as well for me in years.

When the light turned red, they pulled onto 22 and powered up— what else?—the steep hillside. No one was behind me, so I stayed and watched the broad-shouldered car take that hill like nothing. The Caprice gleamed on the slope, gleamed in the tilting sun, and gleamed one last time at the crest before dropping out of sight. Its beautiful sky-blue turned into the silver-blue sky. Oh yeah, that's right, I forgot to tell you: The Caprice was sky-blue. A long time ago, I really loved that car.

WORDS OF WISDOM

[A]nd there is always more to say than I can tell.
 —Dante Alighieri
 Inferno IV, 147
 Translated by Mark Strand

I: Blizzards, Sardines, and the Whole Rest of Garnet's Sign

The ripped speaker cover hung with a dog-eared resiliency from the top corner of Marty Stahl's 1941 Philco radio. Even in the dim kitchen of the upstairs apartment along Route 819, there was still some sparkle left to the tattered fabric, like burlap suddenly laced with gold. As usual, Marty was in brown overalls by six-thirty. He gingerly adjusted the tuning, sipped his coffee, and regarded Tommy Thomas, the Lone Wolf of WDTW Country and Western Radio, just east in Avonmore, PA.

"Boy, he isn't telling his stories today," Marty said, comforted to hear his own voice.

The Lone Wolf announced that the roads of Westmoreland County were so bad that the morning DJ was stuck in his own driveway. "Fact is," the Wolf said, "with all this snow, I'm the only one here in the station. So you'd better watch out! I might start in tellin' some of my daddy's old jokes, the ones what makes the ladies cringe." He let out a raucous laugh loud enough for Marty to turn down the volume. "They're a tad raw, as Momma says, but they rattle the old rafters, and that can't be all bad. Let a little light in that attic, I always say."

"You tell 'em, Wolf," Marty raised his mug to the radio. "Hell, this wasn't supposed to be anything more than a few inches they said last night."

He could tell from the sound of the snow plow rattling his windows that there was plenty of snow, and when he pulled back the curtain over the sink, he blinked at the brilliant landscape, the trees along the highway so laden with it that he couldn't see down to the four corners of Slickville. Every inch of the frozen world was blanketed.

Letting the curtain fall, Marty hummed along with Hank Williams's "Your Cheatin' Heart" as he made his familiar way to the one cupboard. Kneeling and wincing, he pushed the last three cans forward: creamed corn, candied apple rings, and a flat tin of Great Northern sardines.

Rising again at the counter, he adored the blue water on the sardine can, the clipper ship caught in full sail, and the snow-capped mountains in the background. If he were ever there, he thought, that would be a story to tell the retired regulars down at Bentley's. But no, he figured, he could never go that far away. He could never leave Cora.

Reverently, Marty read the sardine label: "Harvested in the bristling waters of the Great North, these legendary sardines are our very best." *Bristling waters*, he thought. He arranged the three cans until they somehow looked right.

Marty's friend Garnet Bentley closed her grocery store early the day before because of the bad weather. Trouble was she never called him. So by the time he had bundled up in his work coat and huffed to town, she was gone. He couldn't receive his little payment in kind for sweeping the four aisles, making close deliveries, and handling the big yellow sign out front. That sign was Marty's favorite job: The top of it announced daily specials, but for the past month now, the whole rest of Garnet's sign was reserved for Marty's own homespun, borrowed, clichéd, or made-up one-liners.

Even though he had to carry sets of notes now, Marty could still come up with the joke or story he needed to best the younger regulars. While Joe Magenta, Buster Higgs, or Curly Griffin read the Greensburg and Pittsburgh papers and tried to out-bullshit one another, Marty waited until the time was just right, flipped through his wallet, and found triggering words like *nuns have good habits* or *whale blubber worth thousands for perfume*. And then he was off, knocking them flat. Once he even saw Garnet double over and stomp her foot in the saw dust she was spreading behind the meat counter. Oh, nothing beat a good story running fluid and smooth in that smoky air, and it was all the better if it left them tearing with laughter.

And his first sign was a success, too. It read, "When you're young, everything comes with a side dish. When you're old, everything comes with a side effect!" After he put those letters up, flipped the switch, and headed for home, he turned to admire the words so often that he appeared to be twirling down Main Street, his unbuttoned jacket flapping behind him like wings.

Marty sipped slowly from the Steelers mug and moved his hand over the three cans, almost touching them, thinking how he could be eating bologna, day-old bread, or cottage cheese, anything better than this if he had made it out of the house sooner yesterday. But his back had ached, the pain numbing his left thigh, and he had to make the trip himself. He couldn't send Cora, his sister, who was sleeping in the next room. She was capable of getting lost or, worse, of making a scene in the store once she got there. Marty pictured Garnet looking up from the cash register, showing a ton of sympathy until her strained smile collapsed with a sigh.

Marty knew that folks looked at Cora as if they were watching an explosion about to detonate. He knew they remembered and could never really forgive her. Not her. Not after what she'd done. Not in a town this small, where joys came and went, but sorrows remained like the buckled hills themselves. Marty could see it in their eyes at the Post Office, at Bentley's, even when he took her to St. Sylvester's on holy days.

No, since the Western Psychiatric Institute in Pittsburgh had released her to his care, Marty had to watch her every move, making sure that she ate right and took her medicine. After all, he thought, no matter how old the two of them got, she would always be his little sister.

The corn gurgled to a simmer. He stood over it and wished for bread, maybe a nice loaf of Cellone's, the kind you had to slice yourself. Italian bread was the best day-old bread because the crust got hard the way he liked it, anyway. As his burning fingers worked the trickier can of sardines, he wished they could just be there, spread across the big plate. He would even give one of them back to God for saving him the pain of turning the impossible manual can opener. It took an oven mitt and a pair of pliers to triumph over the fish.

After kneeling slowly to pick up the dropped mitt, he had an easier time with the candied apple rings, and so he spent his make-shift third wish on wanting back the old days when he worked at the feed store, and Cora taught at the state college. She and her husband, Robert, lived on the Saltsburg Road, by the sawmill, and the three of them had cookouts on warm summer nights. Once Marty remembered that, he had no choice but to see the rest, his face blushing in shame as the Lone

Wolf made a joke and played a laugh track of people shouting, "Amen, Brother Wolf! Amen!"

When the furnace kicked on, the smell of heating oil triggered a dozen thoughts of growing up in Slickville. When they were kids, he helped her lace her skates and then get her balance on Parker's Pond. Later, when Cora won the local Lions' Club scholarship that paid for her first year at Duquesne, he held his suddenly weeping mother as they waved good-bye to her at the bus stop. But Cora never saw them. Her head was already down, her eyes glued to the book in her lap.

He opened the bread box and saw them there: the three old corn muffins wrapped in wax paper. How could he have forgotten them? He crumbled one, resurrecting it into his bowl of creamed corn. It didn't matter that the Lone Wolf had chuckled his way to playing Bill Monroe's "Blue Moon of Kentucky." Taste and thought surged in the kitchen as Marty promised himself that he would have the same breakfast next December twenty-second. This would become his traditional three-days-before-Christmas breakfast, and one day he was going to tell a funny story about it. He went to Cora's church calendar and wrote, "corn, muffins, sardines" inside the square for the day. The items seemed noble next to Saint Abban's name.

Marty dished out Cora's food but knew better than to wake her. She wouldn't eat a thing until later in the day when her soap operas started. He checked his wallet for Garnet's instructions, got dressed, and started down to the store. Ham and pie prices were going on the top half of the sign. Marty knew that. But today, the rest of it was entirely up to him and what the regulars called his words of wisdom.

The biting cold and whipping snow on 819 couldn't keep him from swelling with pride at the space he'd been given. He imagined the big brown boxes of letters in the storage room, and the possibilities unfolded in his blood. What witty thing could he say about the Lions' Club Christmas Dinner or the Lone Wolf playing Santa Claus for the kids at the VFW? What could he say to all of Slickville now that Main Street was suddenly red and white and gold with angels on the streetlights? What could he say?

II: The Gallery of Faces, a Book
by Mark Twain, and the Final Order

Bentley's was warm, and Marty's glasses fogged the second he stepped inside. Garnet was in the back putting freshly baked pies into cardboard boxes and checking names off of her order list.

"Don't have much today, Marty," she called to him, "only these pies, and then I'm closing up shop." She gave her nervous smile and added, "We're supposed to get just a beaut before too long."

"How about the hams and pies, then? I mean, how about the sign?"

She thought it over. "Well, you can scratch the pies. I'm done worrying about pies for this year. And I'm not even sure I'll be opening tomorrow. I hear they're wiping out right and left on Saltsburg Road."

"Okay," he said, taking a chair at the regulars' table by the dry goods aisle. He loved the gallery of faces—the man on the Quaker Oats, the swimmer on the Wheaties, and Marty's favorite, Uncle Ben with what had to be the Mississippi River winding behind him.

Marty jotted down a note to go to the public library and get a book by Mark Twain. Oh, to hold an old book in his hands. That would be a heavy, warm, and certain weight. But then he crossed it out, knowing what a fit Cora would have if she found a book of literature in the house.

"So," Garnet's voice filled the store, "you can go right ahead with the whole sign this time. Make it something nice, something bright, in spite of all this junk hammering us."

Marty tried to think about the sign, but he couldn't concentrate for long with the phone ringing and folks scrambling in for last-minute supplies. Garnet was refusing to bake any more pies or take any more orders. Her hair fallen onto her face, she stood wringing her hands by the dairy cooler when she enlisted Marty to answer the phone, and before he knew it, he was the one saying no to half of Slickville. The order list for the pies was right there on the counter by the cash register, and Marty froze when he saw the last name on it:

Mack Rancelier, 1 apple, 1 mince

He wanted to run, to hurry home up the hill with its familiar hurt warming his legs, but Garnet was standing there talking to him, and he couldn't very well just get up and leave.

Mack Rancelier's name, though, it wouldn't go away. It broke everything loose into a hundred pieces: a flash of Cora's arrest, a flash of Robert's car crash, a flash of the articles in the papers, a flash of the tiny coffin in Saint Sylvester's, the shame of it all flowing down the church steps and flooding the streets.

III: What No One Saw

In July of 1977, Mack Rancelier was a boy of five playing in his back yard as his uncle and father put the roof on the new house on Saltsburg Road.

No one saw Cora next door knife open the letter from the Dean of the state college, the letter denying her tenure and ending her career there. No one knew that her fine teaching evaluations and Chaucer publications had been ignored by a committee of men simply refusing to tenure a woman. No one knew how petty politics and back-stabbing had eaten her alive for the past six years. No one knew that she had been up for three days straight, the last two with a fever-ridden, wailing child. No one heard the anger, frustration, and blood-sorrow burst from her lungs when the child exploded in anguish.

No one saw Cora hold up the child the first time.

No one saw Cora hold up the girl the second time.

No one saw Cora shake her above the crib.

Hammers ringing, the men nailed the new shingles and ascended the pitch of the roof. The day buzzed, and sweat stood out on their foreheads.

No one saw Cora hold up her daughter the third time.

Toy hammer in hand, young Mack flailed away in the sandbox. The sun blistered down.

No one saw Cora hold up Isabella the fourth time.

But Mack did look up when Cora's screened door slammed, and she was in her front yard by the fresh hole Robert had dug for her, the new rhododendron off to one side, its roots covered in burlap.

Her fists balled up in the baby's shirt, Cora flung the heaving child into the hole with a silencing thud. Staggering a few feet forward, she was soon on her knees. A long string of spit dangled from one side of her mouth as she seethed.

Muttering into the lawn, she curled up and passed out, her fists relaxing, her fingers sprawling into the grass.

A few minutes later, Mack and his mother stood over Cora. Eventually, she squinted up at them.

"Cora, honey, what happened? What happened? Where's Baby Isabella?"

Some of the earth had been pushed into the hole. The top of the head and one hand were still exposed.

"I know. I know," Cora sat up. "I'll take those!" She snatched the day's mail from the stunned Mrs. Rancelier. "Your work is forever late!" Cora hissed.

"Mommy, she better plant the big bush, or it ain't gonna grow." Mack tugged at his mother's leg.

"If you want to see me," Cora scolded, "you'll have to see my secretary, Mrs. McGuire." Her eyes were dark flames, shiny, wild, elsewhere. "She has my dossier!"

The word *dossier* jolted Mrs. Rancelier backwards.

"Mommy, is she doin' more of that college talk like you said?" Mack looked up at his mother.

Mrs. Rancelier's trembling hand made its way across the top of Mack's head. Then she took one more step backward, turned, looked down, and buckled over in howling agony.

After the scream shot through the air, the Rancelier brothers ran onto the lawn. Mrs. Rancelier pointed into the hole but then was over it, waving the men away, protecting the child's last privacy.

Her husband, Don, picked her up.

Tools flying from his belt, Johnny Rancelier was on his knees swearing as he brought up the dead infant, her arms hanging.

Cora rose and walked into her house.

Don Rancelier took off his shirt and covered Baby Isabella.

With Mack in his arms, Johnny Rancelier ran back to his brother's house shouting, "I'll call! I'll call!"

Knife in hand, Cora came back out onto the lawn. She turned the garden hose on the Ranceliers.

"Donny!" Mrs. Rancelier grabbed her husband's belt as he lunged for Cora.

Cora crawled away and collapsed by the rhododendron.

When the State Police got there, Don Rancelier was suddenly incoherent, and Trooper Wade Nettles cleared his throat as he slowly pried the dead girl loose from Betty Rancelier's arms.

IV: The Back Porch

Garnet hung up her apron and turned off the kitchen lights. "If Mack don't come in by six, now you leave a note and go on home. Otherwise, do the sign and lock up. Okay, Marty?"

Marty heard himself say, "Okay." And she was out the door and driving away, her noisy Jeep fading down Main Street.

Marty went to the regulars' table and spread his scraps of triggering words like cards in a game of solitaire. He couldn't think of anything new for the sign, so for the time being he resolved to jot himself a personal note: "No pies ever for Xmas." There was simply too much sorrow attached to pies from now on. There could never be a good story to tell about them.

Mack Rancelier stood in front of the cash register. He stomped the snow off his boots and looked right at Marty but didn't so much as blink in recognition.

"Them roads are hell," Mack said. "The pies are thirteen bucks total, right?"

"Sure enough," Marty moved around the counter.

And that was that. The situation washed out the door when Mack shut it behind him. There were no details to write down, no story to tell, no words of wisdom.

Marty opened the bag Garnet had made up for him, and the Hershey bar tasted so good that he had to get a scrap of paper and write it down, but then he remembered the empty sign and felt grounded to the wooden floor.

He stood over the cardboard boxes of letters and was at an even greater loss now. He'd never had the entire sign before. Locking the door and turning off the interior lights, he paced in the shadows, stopping by the Archway cookie rack at the back of the store, shaking his head, and then continuing around the store.

Maybe a little nip of Garnet's Jim Beam might be a good thing, he figured, leaning up against the butcher block. Bottle in hand, he dragged the letters onto the big back porch. In their jumbled chaos, the o's and m's and d's and g's and c's of the world seemed friendly, even promising.

The whiskey was cool and good, then hot and almost talking to him as he pulled on the broad-shouldered bottle, admiring the label's gold ribbon and its important-looking script.

The storm windows were up on the back porch, and he could sit out there and between gusts see over the houses all the way to the base of the mountain. The room was comfortable yet cool enough to store eggs and soda. One more drink, he thought, would hold off the chill and push him along his way.

Last week, the township supervisor's wife gave birth to twin boys. Just a few days ago, Joe Beecher from Fifth Street hit the lottery for five thousand dollars. And yesterday, Mike Dravich pulled a Humvee out of a ditch with his big John Deere tractor.

All of it, all of the possible news or events or messages ran together in his head as if they were somehow connected, even the same thing. They were floating in his mind, in his mind, and he knew that none of it stacked up at last against the howl of the wind with another burning swallow, or the swirling, blinding white, or the cold he knew was out there, always out there and coming down on everyone like a storm front, down, down on everyone as a man named Robert Stinton flew so fast over 819 that day that he flipped through a cow field and exploded his '72 Lincoln into Gilbert Neary's main barn and burned himself out of a place as vicious as this on an otherwise perfect July afternoon.

None of it could unscramble the blizzard of letters that gazed in their waiting to become words. None of it could go into Marty's lungs, where he breathed defeat like poison. None of it could undo the trance he was in staring at the one spot on the bottle where the brown liquor glistened like a girl's eyes. He turned the whiskey again and again, watching the slice of light fade, emerge, and then fade again.

He wrapped up an oblong red pillow in a green blanket and set the small package on the swing-chair across from where he sat. It was close enough that he could rock it with a push from one foot while he rested just a bit, thinking whether or not he'd have one more nip of the bourbon. There was a case of eggs on the swing-chair, too, so he had to be careful. He pushed. Soon, there was that comforting sound, that creaking rocking, that metallic ticking in the room with him. Holding the bottle close, he loved how the sound continued at his control, loved how it meant so much more than words, loved how it told a story all its own.

THE RUN

Tapping his fingers at the kitchen sink and glaring out the window,
Will Wolchak shook his head, unsure who upset him more, people who
humiliated trees, or the Weather Channel meteorologists his wife,
Tammy, had just turned on and had blaring in the living room. The
broadcasters were more excited than usual because of the April Fool's
Day snowstorm that had struck that morning while Tammy was still
sleeping and Will was working in the back section of his garage.

Will looked away, vowing this time to consider the turbulent
question later on, after he got back home from his run. Well, that was,
he stopped himself, if he were still able to make a run with all of the
snow pouring down. He saw himself cracking open a cold Stoney's,
lighting a Royal Jamaica Churchill, and thinking it all the way through
to a conclusion. He took a yellow Post-it note from the refrigerator and
scratched out "humiliated trees" and "weathermen" in shaky lettering.

Humiliated trees and *weathermen*. Because he figured these were the
two biggest problems in his life, Will justified laying the black words on
top of the last ones inside his cigar humidor. The box was nearly full of
Churchills, each wrapped in the gold of loyalty and perfection. Inhaling
the cedar and tobacco sweetness, part of him longed for the absolute
relaxation of a cigar. Part of him was proud that he hadn't smoked one

161

in weeks, inevitably drank too much beer, and obsessed over the accident, no matter what internal debate he had sworn to keep to. But the biggest part of him wished that none of this were happening in the first place, wished that they were still living for birthday surprises, fishing trips, and Sunday dinners.

Why couldn't he have somehow prevented it, seen that Maggie Rae was tired from overtime at the hospital, and made her and Donny Jr. stay for supper and head back to Pittsburgh later? Why couldn't he have stood up to Big Donny, his voice bursting in Will's ears to have Maggie come home now, that she was already late, that he needed his dinner and to talk to her before the nightshift at Westinghouse? *Why?* Why wasn't Will a man of certainty and action like the black-and-white heroes no one knew Tammy lived for during the last eight months? They were never beaten down like this, simply enduring *Post-Gazettes* and Weather Channel updates, slapdash meatloaf, and bedtime reading. Why couldn't he be like the self-possessed John Garfield in *Humoresque*, or the righteous Gregory Peck in *To Kill a Mockingbird*, or the undefeatable Humphrey Bogart in *African Queen*?

After their therapy had ended in early March, it was true, they had made real progress. They began to get out, even if it were only for Tammy's hairdresser appointments or to the Wal-Mart to shop for nothing. They started eating three squares, too, with Will fixing lunches and Tammy planning dinners. But now, he held the fridge door open and fought the chest-deep desire for a beer, a beer to forget the storm, to forget his run for the day, and to forget his neighbor, Crazy Leonard Dove, who had spent the last year shearing, stripping, staining, and shellacking the maple tree in his side yard. Will's anger had mounted with each disappearing part of the original tree. And now, framed in the window, there it stood with eagles and owls perched in the top and middle branches, a bear cub climbing up the lowest limb, and, finally, a misshapen mermaid projecting from its trunk like the masthead of a ship of fools.

That mild October evening when Leonard finished laminating the conquered tree, Will dried dinner dishes with Tammy and couldn't believe the way the man was admiring the lunatic sculpture, smiling up at the tree in exhausted self-satisfaction.

Tammy knelt, putting away pots and pans.

"For Christ's sake, Tam, there ought to be a law, a sort of nature police, or some damned thing. People shouldn't be allowed to just butcher trees like that."

"And it was such a nice tree," Tammy sang into the cupboard, "back when the Roberts had the place. Remember?"

Will couldn't help but remember the tree thirty years ago: Maggie Rae played where now an owl sat fastened into an everlasting tilt. Leonard made a slow, sweeping "perfect" sign with encircled thumb and forefinger, the hand gesture freezing in the air.

"You've got to be kidding me!" Will accused the last of the draining dishes. "And look at that mermaid biker woman with her arms opening as if she's calling all of the retards in the world to come and worship this monstrosity."

"Hey, now, Will," Tammy's voice was disembodied, "remember what Dr. Terbaine said, 'No getting upset, no matter what.' And, honey," her voice was placid with valium, "don't say 'retard.' It's not nice. Why get yourself all worked up? It *is* a free country. A man can do what he pleases with his own tree." Her head was still inside the cupboard. "I saw him down at the Shop and Save. He calls it tree-art."

163

"Tree-art?" Will's throat turned to twisting rope.

"Uh, huh. I'm sure that's it. Says there's tree-art clubs and a magazine and everything." She spoke as if she'd never again have a care in the world. "There's another tree just like it over in Greensburg, up by Saint Emma's Monastery on 819. I know you've seen it."

It wasn't art, and he hadn't seen it, but when she pulled herself up by his arm, he saw her polished red nails, and he smelled the slight muskiness of the Liz Taylor perfume he'd given her. It was the first time since the funerals that she'd done her nails or worn cologne, the first time in a long time that she'd smiled into his eyes, so he said nothing.

"Good," she surveyed the dish drainer. "You've only got the plates and silverware, and then you're good to go. Now, don't ever forget," she playfully added, "I gave you your start in show business." She hung up her towel and left the room.

Her saying the family-famous line about giving him his start in show business was another sign that Tammy was starting to heal, so the words died inside of him while he plopped the last of the silverware into the drawer. He swore, though, that he would think about it later over a beer and a stogie, after Tammy had finished her vodka and tonics and slept to Lana Turner, Audrey Hepburn, or Grace Kelly moving like an angel on the screen.

"Hey, Baker Boy," she called out her nickname for him, "when you're done, it's Spencer Tracey Night on the TCM. First up is *Tortilla Flats*. I'll make some popcorn, and we'll settle in."

"Maybe," he said, reaching for a box of wooden matches.

"Willie," she lit a cigarette and asked with real curiosity, "we *do* have lemons, don't we?"

Now, the light in the kitchen shifted to a darker grey. A can of tuna, the mayonnaise, and an old onion sat on the countertop. In a murky jar, the last two dill pickles waited by the mixing bowl. A chopping block. A fork. A knife. Empty plates. He couldn't imagine possessing the strength to open and drain the tuna, let alone the energy to chop and mix it all. And then the making, the cutting, and the arranging of the sandwiches—that would be Herculean.

Just one of the legion of ice-cold, long-necked bottles that stood at command on the bottom shelf. Inches away. And it would be okay, too, at twelve-ten on a Tuesday, because Tammy caressed a vodka and tonic, the yellow lemon glowing like an exotic caterpillar on the side of the cut crystal glass. It was her fancy touch to make it all right. Drink in one hand, she steadied the remote control with the other, careful not to spill a drop.

He had been working in his basement and garage all morning, restringing his weed trimmer, fixing the engine of his old mower, and changing the oil in his new one. Whistling away in his own world of tools and perfect fits, he surged with the hope of green lawns. In a week, he'd till the garden, and not long after that, he'd get Tammy to help him put in the tomato and pepper plants. But amazingly, during it all, somehow, the snow hit like hell.

Washing his hands, Will shook his head at the whitened transfigured maple as a meteorologist named Bob with no idea of pain belted out the forecast for the hearing-impaired: "And so, for you folks in the east, this is a surprise snow, caused by the sudden clash of a rising jet stream with a mass of frigid Canadian air."

"I guess it takes two to tango, ay, Bob?" A woman named Jane with no idea of misery snickered.

"Right, Jane. At times, there's just not much a body can do."

165

The kitchen window whined in a minor key. Snow. Snow. Snow. The bizarre tree faded and reappeared in the swirling whiteout. As Will lost sight of it for the fourth time, he heard a loud pop, and when the view cleared again, the lower bear-cub branch dangled in front of the mermaid, the dry white inside of the broken limb showing through the half-light. Whether Leonard was in town visiting his daughter or out on errands, Will knew that with his ancient station wagon out on the road somewhere, Crazy Leonard was stuck where he was until the freak storm blew over. Will was also certain that Tammy wouldn't budge now that she had both feet up on the ottoman.

He had worked at Schaller's Bakery in Greensburg for forty-one years and hadn't so much as taken home a box of old doughnuts. But within minutes, Will carried a hatchet, rounded the bushes, and pushed against the wind for the tree. The snow spat from all directions, stinging his chest and face, and he realized that he had forgotten to grab his coat. A wicked gust blew the hatchet out to his side, and for a second, he saw himself as others would see him in his flapping flannel shirt: He was a raving idiot about to attack a lacquered maple in a snowstorm.

He set the rules: If he couldn't break off the branch in ten good whacks, then he was to turn tail for home. The collapsed arm of the tree felt like a gigantic baseball bat in his left hand as he pressured the bear cub down and let the hatchet follow the grain of the wood. He delighted in its resemblance to white albacore tuna. The branch didn't need hard whacks, after all; the dead wood only needed gentle separation. He worked it down, down, until he knelt with the cub in his hands. The mermaid gazed straight at him, but she never saw a thing.

One sweeping, knee-burning deep step at a time, Will walked backwards, wiping out his previous footprints all the way home. He

166

spread newspapers over the picnic table in his garage, caught his breath, and then studied the frozen creature through frosted lenses.

"If I can only . . ." he hoped aloud, tapping the hatchet edge along the side of the figurine. Finally, he eased the cub away from the wood.

He jumped at a sound from inside the house. How on earth would he explain all of this to Tammy? But it was only his trash can lid flying across the backyard.

In seconds, Will reduced the branch to pieces at his table saw. But then he wrapped the bear cub in newspaper and set the bundle in the wastebasket by the tool bench.

He brought the sections of the branch to his basement wood burner. The gas-soaked pile went up with a swoosh, the varnished pieces hissing green, orange, and blue.

Humming to the overture of a movie Tammy must have turned on, Will chopped celery and onions and pickles and green olives so happily that he was sorry to stop and mix the tuna salad. He cut Tammy's sandwich into four triangular pieces, waving the knife like a conductor's wand. Joyously fighting the Lazy Susan, he was on his knees searching for pepper rings.

"Come on, honey," he called, smiling as the bright yellow jar spun from the darkness. "Lunch is ready. And I've got those barbeque chips you like, too."

"Maybe later," she said, her voice smaller than he could imagine.

Tammy sat in silhouette against her window, the four panes beside her fluorescent with snow. She must have pulled back the curtains and finally faced the fact of the storm. The TV was off, and he realized that he had been humming to her radio. The beat-up black box sat at an angle on the sill, its bent antenna against the glass, so she could pick up

WQED in Pittsburgh. That was the position he left her in each night and found her in each morning during those first weeks after the accident. Once, he found her hugging the radio, its barely audible piano filling the room. He tried to repeat his call for lunch, but now his shoulder ached with having cut down the tree branch.

Drink in hand, she blinked at the muted screen with a disgusted vulnerability, taking in the storm's graphics like someone receiving devastating medical news yet remaining too proud to acknowledge it. Will turned away and studied her calendar on the side of the refrigerator: The first two weeks of April were filled in with church events, appointments, and day-trips. She had written "Go, Bucs!" for Monday the seventh, the Pirates Home Opener.

At the front door, he peered through the foggy portal. Snow covered the lawn, sitting deeper in the patches Tammy had readied for reseeding. Snow blanketed his car. Crystals of windshield ice flashed their short-lived fire as the sun peeked through but was swallowed again. He was going to stand there, his sickened stomach promised, until the light broke through at least once more. His watch ticked, but the grayish white never changed. This, he thought, just when he and Tammy were starting to feel better; just when he had no idea at all that it had snowed; just when he had spent the morning singing country and western tunes and dreaming of spinning Tammy on the dance floor at Ron's Tavern, maybe that coming Friday after they got the famous fish fry.

The phone rang five times before Will made the monumental two-step effort to turn around and pick it up.

"Well, Willie. Ain't this all one big bunch of bull hockey? Hey, you folks over there okay?" Crazy Leonard's rapid-fire voice was otherworldly. "I see the lid of your trash can made it clear to the McIntosh tree out back. And I'll tell ya what, I had some damage myself. Lost part of my tree-art out front. Know what I mean?"

"Ahhh," Crazy Leonard answered his own question, "I knew better. I mean, that tree was half-dead before I started in making it art. I knew something was up about ten this morning. I looked out the bay window here, and I said, 'What the livin' shit is that? Not snow again, by God? And it looks like it'll bury us before noon.' So I got my damned wagon to fit in my bastard garage, and I put on a pot of coffee. Hey, I ain't got tickets to the opera, as they say. How about you?"

Leonard stopped as if he had surely said enough to get a response from Will, who sat biting his lip, his mind ablaze with a hundred thoughts but only seeing one thing, Crazy Leonard's moon face with its blinking blue eyes.

"I refuse to buckle under to this unwelcome revisitation of winter, and so, sticking to our regularly scheduled programming, here is the Vienna String Orchestra with Vivaldi's *Spring*," the radio announcer's self-confident voice owned the very air it inhabited as the chorus of triumphant violins and cellos bolted from nowhere to whirl around Will. He heard Tammy sigh. Then she lowered the volume steadily until the only thing he could make out was the breath in the receiver.

Leonard picked up where he had left off: "The TV says this isn't over yet, not by a long shot. I hear Pittsburgh's getting it something terrible. Where on earth did this come from, anyway?"

Stunned, Will's mind rang with the certainty that Crazy Leonard had been at home all along.

"Well . . ." Leonard's voice rose as if he'd been asked a complex question and had a herd of reporters waiting for his insights. "I'd have to say that the bear-cub branch must've been swept away. But what I can't figure out is why your trash can lid didn't blow all the way outta your yard then. Know what I mean?"

Leonard always spoke this way, and it was impossible to tell if he were asking a sincere question or being sarcastic. Hanging up, Will swore he'd give half of his pension to know what the crazy bastard saw.

Part of Tammy's therapy was "to care again" and "to let the world back in." These were the words of gentle Dr. Terbaine. So Tammy got the mail, answered letters, read the morning newspaper, and picked up the phone, or else asked Will who it was when he answered it. Now, though, he watched her bounce from the living room into the kitchen as if she were making her way through a throng of partiers. He heard the tossing of ice into the glass, the removing of the bottle cap, the pouring of the vodka, and then the hissing of the tonic. On her way back, she smiled down the distance of the hallway. In a heartbeat, the Weather Channel filled the house.

"That's *Storms of the Century*, today at four, only on the Weather Channel," the set promised.

"Well, thank you. That sounds like a great idea," she spoke as if making a lunch date with a friend. He heard her hum and could see her program the set reminder. This was her way: If it were no longer possible to ignore something awful, Tammy embraced it as if it had been her idea in the first place.

"Hey, Willie. This old storm's gonna be a while, so why not grab yourself a beer and settle in with me? Robert Mitchum's on in a bit. Then, right after that, there's that special he was saying on storms."

"Yeah. Okay."

"And later on, I'll make us some popcorn. Then we'll have a nice late supper."

"Okay," he forced himself up from the bench.

By the second sip of beer, Will convinced himself that he had every intention of making his run, every intention of slowing them down out there and offering his remembrance of Maggie Rae and Donny Jr. But the storm had hit, and he couldn't drive in all of that wind and snow. He simply couldn't do it, and that was that, he told himself. Besides, sooner or later, Tammy was going to call Robert Mitchum *Bobby*, and then Frank Sinatra *Frankie*, and then Veronica Lake *Vickie*. Sooner or later, Tammy was going to be transformed, laughing and talking and forgetting. And sooner or later, his second and third beers were going to go down like iced silk.

The next morning, Will looked out his bathroom window and saw Leonard searching in the hedgerow between their houses. In one horrific second, he realized that Leonard was staring right back at him. Leonard smiled, pointed at the bushes, shrugged his shoulders, and continued inspecting the snowy branches.

"Jesus," Will shook his head. Was that a friendly smile? Was it knowing? He let the curtain fall back and caught himself looking confused in the mirror.

From the shower, Will heard the Weather Channel booming in the living room. He couldn't recall exactly when it started, Tammy turning into a meteorologist. But his plan had been to let her do whatever she needed to do to work through her sorrow over the accident. He said nothing when she piled meteorology books on the coffee table or kept weather charts on an old clipboard. He said nothing when she recorded local barometric pressures for three weeks straight.

But recently he was strained to the limit. Winter was all but gone, so he drove over to Hanley's Service Station to have the boys take off his treaded tires. The Roadmaster purred, and the air smelled like springtime.

Further east on Route 286, the people hitting the Kiski Flats had their windows down and were driving wildly, exactly as Will had hoped, the speeding fools. He drove over there almost daily since the accident, at first to place flowers, pray with his flashers blinking, and simply say good-bye. But then, after Christmas, he started pulling onto the road, always safely in front of a line of traffic, and then perfectly maintaining the speed limit for the three miles to Saltsburg.

To Will, the ritual of the run was the best internal-debate conclusion he had ever reached. He knew he could slow down the long line of drivers, all barreling into the stretch like bats out of hell. But he lived for that day when somehow he would know, somehow he would feel, that the driver behind him was *the* driver, the heavyset, brown-haired man in bib overalls who witnesses saw flee the scene in a damaged red Ford pickup.

On the drive back from Hanley's, he felt fantastic. Blasting weather forecasts and bygone movie stars were the furthest things from his mind. He had slowed them down, slowed them all down good. But when he walked into the house, Tammy sipped her drink and said, "Boy, Will, wouldn't want to live out in Idaho, great spuds or no. They're calling for a foot of snow there by sunrise, and maybe even more *precip* in elevated sections."

He wanted to explode. How could his wife, Tammy Wolchak of Saltsburg, Pennsylvania, use such terms as *precip* and *elevated sections* to him the moment he came through the door? *How?* How was it possible?

But, of course, he didn't say a thing. Instead he heard himself ask, "Hey, what's on the TCM?"

"I don't know, hun," she reached for the remote. "Let's have a look."

He stood by her, the two of them waiting for the TCM schedule to scroll up on the Preview Channel.

She broke the smoky silence with, "Will, baby, freshen my drink, huh? Come on and settle in with me. Later, I'll heat up those nice soft pretzels in the freezer."

"Sure," he said, taking the thick resplendent glass, its two dead lemons curled under the melted ice.

He could have argued, could have said, "Tammy, put it on the TCM. You know you are, anyway. Why go through the rigmarole of checking with the Preview Channel?" He could have said that. But he loved her fallen shoulders through the volume of the foolish commercials that ran with the ascending program offerings; he loved her green eyes searching through the pain and horror and smallness of what everything in the world had become.

Will freshened her drink. He grabbed a beer. He sat down on the sofa. He said, "You're welcome, baby." He settled in. He tipped his bottle. He did these things. He did them, and he knew them, knew every last second of them. He knew there would be no soft pretzels. Tammy never ate while she was drinking. She was much better at it than he was, much better at sipping and nursing and maintaining and seeing morning into afternoon into evening.

So, he thought, if she wanted to track the lake-effect snowfall over Ontario's eastern shoreline, then let her. If she wanted to nod seriously and draw on a cigarette more deeply while a cool air mass dominated the upper plains, then let her. And, if later, the rivers in her soul were at long last calmed by Polish vodka, and she wanted to watch everything turn out all right with Bette Davis, Greta Garbo, and Liz Taylor inhaling pure light, then let her do that, too. Yeah, he concluded, if she wanted that, *really* wanted that, then let her have it, let her have it all. And God bless Hollywood, and God bless the fucking Weather Channel, and God bless Tammy Wolchak. That is if there were a God to deliver the tortured heart from such anguish.

"Promise me," Tammy was now handing him her grocery list, "only down to the store and back. None of your errands in all of this bad weather. It *has* let up a wee bit," she took a drag and pointed her cigarette to the living room, "but Bobby there just said we may be in for some late-day precip. Okay?"

In the garage, Will looked at the wastebasket holding the bear cub. He looked at Crazy Leonard's house. As he stepped outside, he locked the door.

"Gee . . ." Leonard was standing beside his car, a lurching bronze dinosaur of a 1976 Ford Gran Torino that looked like a cruise missile in flight. "I can't say as I ever saw you lock that door before, Will?"

"Oh, hi, Len," Will tried not to act surprised. "Yeah, the wind's been knocking hell out of it."

Leonard lifted then tilted his head as if, despite the slight downgrade, he could see past his neighbor by sheer determination alone. "Well," he swung into his car, "I'll shoot over this after and have a little look-see at them hinges and that lock for you."

Leonard patiently sat at his fuzzy steering wheel while Will brushed and scraped his car.

All the way down the mountain into Saltsburg, Will saw Leonard looming behind him as the Loyalhanna River churned like a black train through the trees far below the slope.

Tammy was sending him for soup bones. "Come on, Willie," she had said, "let's make up a big old pot of vegetable beef and beat this storm to the punch." He knew it had to be Bobby's or Jane's suggestion.

Will was sorry he had chosen to stand and wait as the butcher trimmed and sawed and wrapped away because here came Leonard, ambling toward him, picking an item off the shelf, scrutinizing it, then putting it back in a different spot. Behind him, a clerk shook his head.

"This look good to you?" Leonard held up a whole chicken. "Looks about this side of gray to me, it does."

"I'm not sure, Len. I suppose it's okay. I've got no complaints about the food here. We've always been satisfied."

"Uh huh . . . I see." Leonard absorbed this as if he were pondering scientific data. "Well, when things don't look right to me, I walk right on by and go to the next thing. Know what I mean, old Will?"

Will wanted to shout, "No, you crazy prick! What the hell *do* you mean? Look, did you see me? If so, I'm sorry. I didn't mean to do it. I've still got the bear cub wrapped in paper. You can have it back. But I'm sorry. I don't know what came over me."

Leonard tossed the chicken into the case and gave Will a bonding look that said they were both well above being duped by post-dated poultry.

Then, in the glaring light of the meat aisle, it hit Will: The only thing worse than Crazy Leonard Dove seeing him attack the tree was Crazy Leonard Dove wanting to be his friend.

"So, Willie, what's on tap for us this after?"

His new friend followed Will aisle to aisle.

"Aren't you going to get any groceries today, Len?"

"Naw. I got all that I need. Know what I mean?"

Will nodded yes, but, of course, he hadn't the slightest clue.

Out of the parking lot, across the Kiski Bridge, and back up the mountain they went, Will leading the way. Leonard slowed down, beeped, flashed his lights, and put on his directional when they passed Ron's Tavern. But Will kept on driving.

Back in their driveways, Leonard yelled over, "Hey, Will, I thought we agreed to stop for a brew at Ron's? What gives?"

"Some other time, Len."

"Huh?" He looked confused. "Well," he smiled, "that's okay. But remember now, I'll be over later this after, like I said about that door."

Back inside, Will wanted to tell Tammy everything. But he said, "I'm taking that garbage in the garage out to the dump. With this wind, I can't set it out for tomorrow, and I don't want it where it is anymore. It smells."

"I don't smell anything, Will."

"That's because you smoke, honey. That kills your sense of smell."

Will had the three bags in his trunk and was out of his driveway in no time, his heart pounding in his neck as the rearview mirror stayed empty.

Riding back from the dump, Will felt free. The bear-cub bag fell into an infinity of black garbage bags just like it. Will had seen it with his own two eyes.

The roads were pretty dry, and with all of the other drivers whizzing by, he pledged to make it back out later for a run. Singing "Sweet Dreams" along with the radio, he swore he'd talk Tammy into the fish fry this Friday night at Ron's. They'd dance. Then they'd go bowling on Saturday and somehow run into all of their old friends. Will would roll a perfect game. The lanes would erupt. His name would hang in triumph above the alleys. They'd go to church on Sunday. The Highway Diner afterwards for peach pie and coffee. Then they'd drive to Pittsburgh for the Pirates game. They'd sit in box seats and drink cold Iron City beers. Will would catch a foul tip. He'd give it to Tammy with a kiss. Their section would roar in a wave of applause.

The house was silent. Still in the cellophane, the beef bones lay on the countertop. Nothing else had been unpacked. He heard the distant strains of a cello. The deep click of ice in a crystal glass. The sigh of her butane lighter. The snap of her cigarette pack. The tobacco itself turning to ash on the first drag.

Bottle in hand, Will marched back to the Buick, never seeing Crazy Leonard pausing out of his side door. Carefully taking the usual back roads through the empty fields, Will was on his way around the mountain. The beer beaded up in the cup holder, but he promised himself it was for later, just a drop to celebrate.

Two more hills, and he would arrive at the intersection of King's Road and 286, so Will let himself remember Maggie Rae. He smiled at how hard he and Tammy had to work to get pregnant.

First, her regular doctor said it was only a matter of bad timing. So they made love in the early morning darkness before his shift at Schaller's and her day at Valley Savings. They made love during her lunch hour, both of them once breathless in the back of his bread truck, then Will skidding all over the roads to make up time on his deliveries. And they made love in the nighttime, staggering the hours later and later until one morning at four-thirty Will couldn't tell if Tammy were being passionate or having a seizure.

Next, a specialist said it was only a matter of bad positioning. So they made love upside down, sideways, backwards, and inside out. They made love in the basement, in the living room, in the kitchen, in the bathroom, and in the attic.

Then, another specialist said it was only a matter of Tammy eating Italian food and Will getting into shape. So she ate artichoke hearts soaked in Sicilian vinegar, and he jogged up and down the mountain. She ate shrimp scampi; he did push-ups in the garage. She drank Bardolino, gained ten pounds, and still wasn't pregnant; he fasted altogether, did sit-ups in the basement, and swore his penis would fall off, crawl away, and come back with a lawyer.

Then, as they were getting ready to adopt a child, Tammy woke up, got sick, went to her regular doctor, and was told, "See? It was only a matter of bad timing."

Maggie Rae was a green-eyed girl, like her mother. She never minded being an only child, occupying herself for hours, coloring, reading, climbing that tree, or practicing her clarinet later on in the fourth grade. Her picture was on page three of the *Saltsburg Record* one night when she graduated from Pitt's School of Nursing. She became an intensive care specialist and was promoted to co-director of her nursing unit three weeks before she died in the head-on collision.

Will stopped at the intersection, the car rocking onto its back tires solidly like a race horse in its starting gate. He was about a quarter mile west of the reduced-speed zone. As usual, he studied the western horizon, waiting for a line of cars to come flying over the ridge.

Will pulled out in front of an old Cadillac Fleetwood that floated up to tailgate him instantly. He saw in his rearview mirror the young woman driving. She was alone, her face beautiful but embittered. As she slapped the steering wheel, she mouthed out, *Fuck!*

She fumbled to light a cigarette and then tapped it against her sideview mirror. Her car was so broad, and the road was suddenly so level that Will couldn't tell for sure how many vehicles rode behind them. He guessed at least five or six. This was going to be a good run.

The woman in the Fleetwood tossed her cigarette; it sparked orange and red on the roadside. She put another one in her mouth but didn't light it as Will led the procession along the Kiski Flats and down the sweeping curve to the bridge and across the river to Saltsburg. Will wanted to make another run, so he turned around at the Citgo, stealing a sip of the beer as he circled the vacant gas pumps.

When he was back up on 286, he saw the shadows fall across the highway, and he knew that there would be no fish fry on Friday, no dancing. No bowling on Saturday, no church on Sunday. No pie and coffee, no Pirates game. No hot dogs, foul balls, or kisses in the stands. He knew it. But he could make his runs and live in that holding pattern, that powerful, steel, humming bliss, and he could remember Maggie Rae, Donny Jr., and Tammy, too, the way she used to be, back before Lizzie Taylor and Paulie Newman made up in the end of *Cat on a Hot Tin Roof,* and Tammy cried that life was great and awful at the same time, and wouldn't he please tell her why it had to hurt so much in your heart once you saw it.

A mile outside of Saltsburg, a farm tractor was slowing traffic to a crawl. Will gazed at the cars in front of him and wasn't prepared for the sudden sight of Leonard Dove standing by his steaming station wagon along the other side of the road. And worse, Leonard's head jolted back when he spotted and waved to Will, who now had no choice but to wave back, pull over, and put on his flashers.

"I saw you pull out your driveway," he said hopping into the car, "and I figured we'd head down the bar and have that beer before I fixed your garage door. I saw you hit the shortcut, but my old gold bullet here started in sputterin', and I couldn't keep up. Think it's a belt." He looked around the interior of the car, spotted the opened beer, and sang in proud praise, "Well, I see you already beat me to that beer, anyways."

"Yeah," Will said. "I shouldn't have opened it. I was saving it. But it's all yours if you'd like."

"Hey, thanks, old Will," Leonard sipped the bottle. "What say we head over the tavern and shoot some pool? He's got one of them big-screen TV's up front now, except it's kind of small, and he's got two albino deer up over the back bar, too, right by the Elvis collection. One of the albinos is sort of brown, but they're both still a sight to see."

"What about your car?"

"Ah, I'll call my daughter when we get there. She'll leave a note for Chuckie, and he'll scoot over after work. No problem. He'll get her to turn over. Besides, he owes me since I'm makin' some tree-art at his place."

Will swallowed hard and then swung around to head back toward Saltsburg. He would take the long way back up the mountain. He refused to share the back roads or any other official part of his run with anyone, least of all Leonard Dove.

"Sip?" Leonard offered the bottle to Will.

"No, Len. You go ahead."

Taking a deep pull on the bottle, Leonard considered the snowy landscape outside his window and then took in the lush blue interior of the Roadmaster. Regally nodding, the crazy man appeared completely satisfied with the world around him.

"You know, Will," he motioned back toward his abandoned car, "I don't mean to spoil our good mood or anything, but right where I broke down, somebody left flowers. I seen two bunches of them, colorful ones. Know what I mean?"

Will wasn't listening because he realized that he was being tailgated by a red pickup. It was a brand new Chevy, and a woman with short blonde hair was at the wheel, so he knew it could never be *the* truck. Still, he went exactly the speed limit and led it and the three cars behind it through the half-mile that remained of the Kiski Flats.

As if he'd been handed life's microphone itself, Leonard was off and rambling about the right way to strip and varnish a maple tree and the various debates that raged over it in the world of tree-art. It was nonsense, but it couldn't detract from the beauty of the minivan honking its horn two cars back or the flashing headlights in Will's mirrors. Next, Leonard was inviting Will and Tammy to come along sometime and help with Chuckie's tree, maybe this coming Sunday when they were going to decorate the main branch with a climbing family of raccoons. It was absolute bullshit, but it couldn't take away from the perfection of these last seconds of slow descent into Saltsburg, Will gripping the wheel tightly, keeping his eyes straight ahead, and never once flinching from the exact completion of his mission.

THE MAN WITHOUT ANY SINS

for Jack Giles

"Maybe they were better at it than we were," Kendall said,
"but everybody's a secret from everybody else."
    —Frederick Busch
    "Bread"

It all started last Wednesday over at my Lakeshore Bar and Grill when Manny McMahan stopped in with his secretary, Bonnie Polanski. She's got legs up to her neck as they say, and sure enough, the damned regulars stared her up and down in her gray work suit. For crying out loud, they looked like a bunch of dogs drooling out of car windows. But as soon as she turned around, the sad bastards bowed their heads to their drinks and smokes and were as innocent as kids kneeling in pews. Yeah, right.

Well, Manny was quiet like always, drinking his CC and ginger, and Bonnie ordered a Bombay and tonic. Only in her case, she likes the first one in a coffee cup because like that, she can pretend she's not drinking at three o'clock in the afternoon. I studied psychology courses at Oswego State about thirty years ago before I had to quit and take over my father-in-law's place here, and with all the time I've been bartending, too, I'd like to think I've got a grip on why folks do what they do. Well, I used to think so, anyway.

Truth be told, the story's kind of a family feud going back decades, or at least that's how it played in Pete O'Connell's mind, and that's why he was always lying in wait for Manny. See, Pete's uncle was John O'Connell, the writer. Maybe you've heard of him. The O'Connell family still has the onion farm out on the Hall Road in Scriba. In the forties and fifties, John kept to himself as much as possible. He raised onions and lettuce with his father and uncle, and he spent his nights writing in the farmhouse out back. Over the years, he published two novels, one called *Faith in You* in 1948, and one called *The Shoreline* in 1955. He made some money and got some attention from the critics. But I guess that was about it. Now, though, the funny thing is there's a cult more or less with the local writing students. They study his books, have a conference out there, and celebrate his birthday every year.

Anyway, about a year ago, a couple of the kids from SUNY went and found out that Pete was the nephew of John O'Connell. I had to laugh. Our barfly Pete causing so much excitement? I mean, he was pretty much a loser: He quit school because a teacher tried to help him; he left his wife for two weeks because she asked him where he was going in a rain coat when the sky was bluer than blue; he even worked for me some time ago, and he up and quit because I wouldn't give him Thursday afternoons off.

"Thursday afternoons?" I asked. "Who needs Thursday afternoons off, Pete? You a doctor or something?"

And that was it. He was out the door, looking like he had someplace to go and was already late.

Then I looked up from the paper one day and saw him at his regular stool like he never left in the first place. I asked him, "You got something to say?" I figured he would want to apologize. But not Pete.

All he said was, "Hey, Joe, the booze is always sweeter on this side of the bar."

Ah, I gave him a beer on the house and forgot about it. If he wanted to be a make-believe mystery man, that was his thing.

Well, these two writing students wanted to interview Pete, and I let them get all set up in the back booth with a tape machine and everything. They didn't have him back there more than five minutes, and *bingo!* He flags down one of the regulars, old Paulie Bosco, and tells him he needs a fresh beer. You should've seen it, Pete trying to turn Paulie of all people into a frigging waiter. So, Paulie scratches his bald head and says, "Pete, you want a beer, get off your ass and get a beer. It's that simple. No hocus-pocus."

Anyway, thing is, no one could hear the students' questions or Pete's answers. We all tried to pretend we were paying attention to the CNN over the bar, and I only caught hell from Paulie when I tried to lower the volume on the set. But after the students closed up shop, Pete snuck out the back door and disappeared for days. And seriously, none us had a clue where he went, not even Lorraine, that angel he married.

That next Saturday night, all hell was breaking loose, and we were packed to the gills with college students, drink specials, and a band playing, too, and Pete came back, somehow found his regular spot, and sat there sipping a Bud. A few times, he went over to the phone booth and mumbled into the receiver. He must have forgotten that the phone had been dead for a few weeks.

I'll bet he thought he had us going good, but I knew better. See, Stan Munson, my chips-and-snacks guy, he was making deliveries out east, and he spotted Pete at the bar of the Hannibal Hotel, said he was eating the meatloaf special with his head down all the while. So, the plain truth was that Pete took off from here after the interview, and then he holed-up in the damned Hannibal Hotel for about a week. And another thing that he didn't know I knew was that the college kids who interviewed him couldn't use anything he said.

"Oh, Joe," one of them had told me, "it was obvious to us that Pete hardly even knew his uncle. At any rate, he didn't know much about John O'Connell's writing."

"Yeah," the other one said, "we told him thanks, but we were going to use other places for our research. I think he took it kind of hard. I hope he didn't say anything to you. I mean, we *were* polite to him."

"No, no," I told them. "Not to worry. He's just like that. He puts on a good act. He can even still dupe some of the regulars."

I poured them a pitcher of Labatt's on the house. They were good kids. What the hell? Still, it was pitiful to see a guy so knee-deep in all of these mysteries that didn't exist.

But I wanted to tell you about all of those years ago, how this damned thing goes back to what happened over at Saint Pat's church on West First. See, Manny McMahan's uncle was the pastor there. He was one of these hard-nosed, no-nonsense Irish priests. His church, convent, and school ran like the sun, moon, and stars, and nobody crossed him. Well, one Saturday afternoon during confession, this old-timer came in and told Father McMahan that he simply had no sins that week.

"What?" The priest wasn't used to such things.

According to Manny, who was a kid there with his mom, you could hear a pin hit the marble floor when the man repeated in his thick Irish brogue, "I'm quite sure of it, now, Father. Search me soul, I don't have a sin to say this week at all."

The man's voice was small, Manny said, tragic, and even apologetic.

Father dragged the man from his side of the confessional, rushed him through one of the massive front doors, and booted him down the inside steps, yelling, "And don't come back in here until you *do* have some sins!"

Manny said that the men behind him bit back their explosive laughter, but the ladies in front of him stood so still that he saw the cross from one of their rosaries freeze in the air.

The rest of the story goes like this: John O'Connell, the reclusive writer, had been coming into town to attend mass at Saint Pat's. He went there when he was a boy, and now he was returning to the church. In one of his books, there's the story of the boy who has a vision in an Irish-Catholic church, and folks in Oswego knew he was writing about himself and Saint Pat's. At any rate, more and more after mass, he started having these religious discussions with Father McMahan. People saw them walking and talking, their voices rising and falling. And you know, they spoke with passion, sure, but they were never hostile or anything. But Manny said all of that changed when word got around that the man tossed out of church was John O'Connell's uncle, the onion farmer Michael O'Connell.

Now, Manny was an altar boy then, and one bitter, snowy day he was serving the early morning mass. This was a few months after the old guy got the holy heave-ho. Manny said it was like any other winter morning mass: The poor faithful were thawing out in the back; a regular or two was scattered on either side in the middle; and then you had your two rows of nuns up front.

The darkness was starting to lift outside through the stained-glass windows, and mass was well underway when the side door creaked open. There was the sound of whipping wind, and in walked John O'Connell, who blessed himself and knelt down with everybody watching. Manny saw it all out of the corner of his eye, his knees aching on the altar pillow as he dared not turn around. He saw his uncle pause from his Latin chanting and fix the late arrival in a deadly stare. The guy hated disruptions. Better to freeze to death out in Ontario's wrath than to interrupt Father Francis David McMahan during the Eucharistic prayers. Everyone knew that.

After Manny and his uncle genuflected and walked to the sacristy, Father went right to the peephole that came out over the shoulder of the Virgin Mary at the side-altar devotional candles, and he squinted out to see John O'Connell, now in a back row, praying the rosary.

Father tightened his lips, shook his head, and went out to talk to the writer. Manny stood tiptoed at the peephole as the two men argued, weaving their way back up the center aisle toward the front of the church. Manny said he could hear them straining to maintain forced whispers, but Father's tone of voice remained harsh all the way back up to the front doors. His were the last words as the writer turned and disappeared.

Here's the real thing, now: Later that same day, John O'Connell shot and killed himself, first in the right foot, and then in the face. Some said it was a horrible freak accident; others said it was clearly suicide. He used an antique Italian pistol. People said he cherished the firearm and knew exactly how it worked, that there was a two-page description of it in one of his books. Others said that the gun was faulty, that it had gone off before in his hands, and he really shot himself by accident while trying to clean it. They said there was a shovel by his foot, and he tripped over it. Funny how a mystery starts up, huh? Either way, his Uncle Mike was the one who found him in the barn sprawled over bags of that year's onions.

Manny said that when he got older, he finally worked up the nerve to ask his uncle about it all. Was the man without any sins Michael O'Connell? Were the two men fighting over him being kicked out that Saturday at confession? Or did he and John O'Connell argue over something else, maybe something the writer had believed or written?

"He never would tell me," Manny once said. "He gave up nothing."

So, last Wednesday, when Manny came in with Bonnie Polanski, Pete was over at the jukebox pumping in quarters for his usual Sinatra songs. In that sly way of his, he walked over to Manny and asked, "So, what you drinking today, Manny?"

"CC and ginger, like always, Pete," Manny kept looking at the TV, and you could see that he was losing his patience already.

"CC?" Pete grabbed his Bud, took a sip, and appeared to be deep in thought. "I wonder how much of that stuff somebody could down and still be able to walk up to Bridge Street and back without falling over or puking?"

A few of the guys really pricked up their ears at that one.

"What?"

"No way, Pete."

"I don't know," Manny tapped his cigarette and finally looked at Pete. "How much CC *could* somebody drink and still do all that?"

"Well, I've been doing some research on the very topic, and I say *I* could drink a fifth of it and still make it up to Bridge and back."

"Time limit, Pete?" Manny turned to take the challenge.

Bonnie Polanski stiffened, touched his arm, and made a little click with her tongue.

Pete never blinked.

Bonnie let out a nervous laugh.

The regulars spun around on their stools.

"Ninety minutes," Pete stared him dead in the eye.

"Hell you can, Pete. You're nuts," I told him. "No one can hold that much booze in ninety minutes, and I'm not letting you try."

"If I don't use *your* booze, Joe, you ain't what they call liable. That's the law." And there he was, Pete being the expert in all of the things none of us could even imagine.

As the *Lucy* rerun glowed on the TV, Pete was back from his house and at the curb behind the wheel of his old Chrysler Newport. He was out there sipping buttermilk. He had his window rolled down, so everybody in the Lakeshore could see him plain as day. He spent five minutes steadily chugging the stuff. This was his big secret: Coat the stomach with buttermilk long enough to hold off the whiskey.

The official witness between the door and the curb was Andy Magano. He stuck his head in through the archway and gave the updates. The guy took his job so seriously that he was the only one who didn't have a dime in on the bet.

"Here's the bottle," he set the CC on the bar, and a couple of us idiots inspected it like evidence before the high commission, for Christ's sake.

"Okay, it's the real deal," Manny was satisfied.

"Yep," Paulie Bosco looked through the bottom of his trifocals, "that seal's perfect."

"Manny, can I talk with you?" Bonnie tried to get his attention.

"Not now, Bon," he handed the bottle to Andy and took a few steps toward the door to get a clear shot at Pete.

The funny lady on TV didn't seem so funny for once, and I had that weird feeling that I'd lived through the moment a thousand times before. I looked at the pot of three hundred and some-odd dollars, and I knew then and there that I should have called the cops.

A *Green Acres* and nearly a *Get Smart* later, Andy announced the obvious: "Hey, Joe, he's all done." He brought the empty bottle in. Sure enough, not a drop left in it.

They passed it around, the regulars bowing their heads in reverence, and Bonnie drew a breath just holding the thing. The place filled with fear and wonder at the same time.

"Okay," Manny yelled out the door, "so you drank it! Now, you gotta make it up to Bridge and back without falling down or puking, you brain-dead shit!"

"Oh, Manny," Bonnie said.

"Hey, it was *his* bet," Manny said, and some of the others nodded to agree.

Pete's car door screeched open, and he started staggering up East Seventh. I don't know why, but nobody thought to go along with him, you know, the way people in lifeboats tag a distance swimmer. I guess we were too amazed that he polished off the fifth. But one at a time, we drifted out of the bar and congregated on the corner.

Bonnie took off her glasses and squinted, "What the hell's he doin' now, Manny?"

"I got no idea."

None of us did. We studied the street, but there were people and cars, and we were losing sight of him.

"I see him!" Paulie Bosco shouted as if his vision had been suddenly restored.

"Me, too," somebody else said.

"Yeah," Manny said, "but the fool's crossing Bridge Street. Look!"

"Oh," Bonnie sang, "I'll bet ya he's only going home to sleep it off."

"Yeah," I hoped, "he lives over there on Eighth."

We stood like morons, nodding away.

"Hey, look, folks," I said. "Let's go back inside. Drinks on the house. I'm giving you all back your money, and we'll forget this fucking thing ever happened. Pete might be a brick shy of a full load, but he's too shit-pitiful to rob over a dumb bet we never should've taken in the first place."

The music was playing and the drinks were flowing and Manny and Bonnie even sprung for some Pizzas from Vona's. It was a regular party. Sure, I heard the sirens, but I was having so much fun that I never thought in a thousand years there was a connection to Pete. Later when there was a lull, and people were sitting down, Zip Ciappa came in all flushed and huffing that Pete had shot his wife.

"Four times," he caught his breath. "Four goddamned times, Joe." His voice broke completely as Bonnie helped him to a stool. "He shot the girl four fucking times."

I could feel them all look at me like I had some sort of magical solution.

"Jesus, Zip. That's awful. I mean, we saw Pete park his car out there earlier, but he didn't come in or nothing. He hasn't been in all day."

"Yeah," Manny said, "I saw him, too. I figured he was gonna come in and bust balls on me like always. But he never showed."

"He just walked down the street," Paulie Bosco said.

I was proud of what liars we were.

Bonnie walked off to the ladies' room, her mouth frozen open.

It happened so fast, like something that was bigger than all of us.

And Zip swallowed the whole thing. He settled in with his Johnny Walker on the rocks.

Manny and Bonnie were leaving, and I walked them outside. She got in the car and shut the door.

"Hey, Man," I asked him, "is she gonna be all right?"

"No problem, Joe. The cops will probably be around because his car's still there. But it's a simple enough story to stick to. We saw him, but he never came in." Then he drew a deep breath: "Christ, what was that stupid jerk thinking?"

An hour or so later, the college crowd started coming in, and the place was all music and pool and pinball. I was so happy to see those noisy bastards that I gave away the first few pitchers or beer. Then I drew myself a draft and added a drop of Jack Daniels. You know, just for color.

At eleven, I snuck back to the office to catch the Syracuse news from the little set on top of the old books. She was going to pull through. Then I eased the door shut, and the broadcaster told me personally, "But Mr. O'Connell was pronounced dead on arrival at the Oswego Hospital." He said it once, but I heard him a hundred times.

When I closed the place, I took the empty bottle of CC and broke it, scattering the pieces in two different bags of trash. Then I wiped down the side of Pete's car, the place where I saw Andy Magano rest his hand when he was out there being our official witness. Jesus, my heart was pounding. I thought the whole world saw me working that rag.

Thursday morning, two Oswego cops showed up at the house. They asked a few questions, took a few names, and said they'd call me if they needed anything else. When I got to the Lakeshore, some other cops were photographing and towing Pete's car. When they raised it up, I saw that spent container of buttermilk glint for a split second on the dashboard. *Why?* Why couldn't I have remembered to get rid of it? Would it mean anything? Did anybody else touch it? Would they print it? My heart raced, but I waved out the bay window at one of the cops, anyway.

I climbed the steps of Saint Pat's Saturday and stood in line for confession. There were three older women in front of me, their faces grave and severe. I wondered what the hell they had to be so sorry about, what sins could be inside such tender hearts. As the line inched along, I convinced myself more and more that I would tell the priest the whole thing.

When the confessional door slid open, I began with the usual, "Bless me, Father, for I have sinned . . ."

"Yes," he said, "go on."

I made up some petty crap about swearing around my neighbor's kids.

"Anything else?" He waited patiently. I couldn't even hear him breathing.

I wanted to say, "Yes, there is. There *is* something else. What makes people do the stupid shit they do to hurt each other? How do you even know there *is* a God? Or that Jesus was his son? How are you so sure we aren't spinning alone in space, shooting each other in the stomach, hips, and legs? And can't we tell each other that we're sorry for our sins? Isn't *that* enough?"

I wanted to say it all. I wanted to tell him about my lie, about Manny and his uncle the priest, about Pete and his uncle the writer, about the man without any sins, about the bet, the buttermilk, the fifth of CC, and the shooting. But where would I start? So instead, I said, "No, Father. That's it. Thanks for listening."

193

"Listening to what?" He gave a chuckle through the wooden mesh. "The rest of my afternoon should go so smoothly." He gave me my penance and slid the divider closed.

As I knelt there, I heard the divider open on the other side of the confessional, and a woman began to weep. I couldn't hear a word, but her misery surrounded me in the darkness of the booth.

I sat in my car across the street and watched Bonnie Polanski come out, dab her eyes, scoot down the steps, and head down First Street.

I took the long way home, so I wouldn't drive by her. I wondered what would happen to us. Was it all over? Was it just beginning? Were we in trouble? Would I lose the bar? Would we go to hell? Was there a hell to go to in the first place?

I started thinking about Mike O'Connell, the man without any sins, the one Father McMahan must've booted out of church all those years ago. What happened that afternoon? Did he ever go back to Saint Pat's? Maybe he crossed West First Street and went to Stone's candy store. Maybe he entered the sweet-smelling shop and bought a little bag of fresh popcorn. Maybe he returned to the church but stood there unable to go back inside and give the priest a piece of his mind. Maybe he made it all the way to the front doors themselves.

When I parked in my garage, I sat there and thought and thought about it until I saw it, really saw it.

In my mind, he shook his head, walked down the steps, and made his way across the lawn between the church and the school. He made it up the hill to the park. The light broke through the trees. On a bench, he watched some kids run off. He thought of them as beautiful but laughing hearts that fade away.

He wanted to get up and leave but thought to sit a moment more in the cold sun. He saw the priest walk from the church to the rectory, and the farmer smiled but was unseen. He threw some popcorn to the birds in front of him, tossing piece after piece until the bag was gone, until the last of the pigeons came down from the trees.

About the Author

Poet and fiction writer STEPHEN MURABITO is a Professor of English at the University of Pittsburgh's Greensburg campus. His short stories have appeared in such places as *North American Review*, *Antietam Review*, *Sou'wester*, and *Paper Street*. He is the author of the poetry chapbook *A Little Dinner Music* (Parallel Press, 2004) and three other full-length books of poetry—*The Oswego Fugues*, *Communion of Asiago*, and *Lowering the Body* (all from Star Cloud Press). He is also the author and editor of the composition textbook *Connections, Contexts, and Possibilities* (Prentice Hall, 2001). He lives in Saltsburg, PA, with his wife, April, and their four children: Angie, Stella, Toni, and Sebastian.

www.ingramcontent.com/pod-product-compliance
Lightning Source LLC
Chambersburg PA
CBHW030521020726
47494CB00004B/1187